ROOM SERVICE & MURDER

The Madness and Murder Mysteries, Book 2

MELISSA BALDWIN

Books by Melissa Baldwin

Cozy Mystery

Poison in Paradise: a tropical romantic mystery

Movie Scripts & Madness (The Madness and Murder Mysteries #1)
Room Service & Murder (The Madness and Murder Mysteries #2)

Romantic Comedy & Chick Lit

On the Road to Love (Love in the City #1)
All You Need is Love (Love in the City #2)
From Runway to Love (Love in the City #3)
Pushing Up Daisies Collection (Love in the City short story)

One Way Ticket (written with Kate O'Keeffe)
Friends ForNever (From Gemma Halliday Publishing)

An Event to Remember (Event to Remember #1)
Wedding Haters (Event to Remember #2)
Not Quite Sheer Happiness (Event to Remember #3)

See You Soon Broadway (Broadway #1)
See You Later Broadway (Broadway #2)

About Room Service & Murder

There's never a dull day working in the hotel industry. Drug busts, arrests, plenty of clandestine escapades, and parties so wild they'd put fraternities to shame. The last thing Casey Cooper expected was to walk into a guest room and discover the lifeless body of her friend.

Though all signs point to a self-inflicted death, Casey doesn't believe it. On a truth-seeking journey to find justice for her friend, suddenly everyone looks like a suspect. Could it be the former child actress, the over-worked assistant, a long-lost relative, or even the delicious new manager who always seems to be distracting Casey from her mission to find her friend's killer?

Can Casey find the truth before the body count rises and she becomes the next victim?

Copyright © 2019 by Melissa Baldwin

Cover design by Sue Traynor

Formatted by The Letterers Collective

Print ISBN: 978-1093306521

Version: 04-08-2019

I dedicate this book to my sweet mother-in-law, Sandra,

who loves to curl up with a good mystery.

Thank you for raising such a great son!

Chapter One

I've seen some crazy stuff during my years of working in the hotel industry. Drug busts, arrests, plenty of mistresses, and parties so wild they would put fraternities to shame. However, never in a million years would I have thought I would ever walk into a guest room and discover the lifeless body of my friend.

J find it so intriguing when guests choose to stay at our hotel under an alias, especially when they aren't real celebrities. There have been numerous occasions when I've wanted to remind these guests of this sad but true fact. Seriously.

Hello, *Ms. Ruby Carson*. Who do you think you're kidding? We all know you're the infamous former child star Mikenzie Bronsyn, and you haven't done anything in the business since you were a pre-teen. Now you're pushing thirty, and most people don't remember you or your acting days. Well, except for how you spend your fortune and steal the hotel dishes and linens. And about that ... why would you want sheets that have been used by thousands of people anyway? Just think about the stories those sheets could tell if they could. Ew. The thought makes me throw up in my mouth. Besides the ick factor, I would think your Malibu mansion would have the finest million-thread-count sheets adorning beds that have never been slept on.

Oh, and news flash—it doesn't make your alias any more believable to name-drop your credentials in conversation.

I could say this out loud ... instead, I stand still in the grand, sprawling lobby of our hotel, smiling with my best-staff-member-in-the-world attitude. As the new director of customer relations, I bite my tongue. As usual. The truth is, I've only been in my position for a few days, ever since the former director, Joelle, was fired for having an inappropriate relationship with our hotel manager, Colton. As soon as the news of their fling got out, it spread like wildfire, and Colton and Joelle were both fired.

I know it seems a little extreme because there aren't actually any set rules about dating co-workers or people in management. And of course they aren't the first two people in our industry to be caught in this type of situation. But when your wife is the sister of the regional vice president, a sordid, scandalous affair seals your fate. I doubt Joelle will ever work in the hospitality industry in California—or the whole country—again. People talk, and Colton's wife's family has a lot of power. Coincidentally, no one has heard a peep from Joelle, so maybe she was already run out of town ... or sent somewhere wearing cement shoes. Yikes, that thought sends chills through my body.

"Did you ever see that movie? It was nominated for several awards," Mikenzie, or "Ruby," says, pulling me out of my internal monologue. She flips her long golden hair extensions over her shoulder. They hang down her back, and I notice a few strands of pink and blue in the mix. I would love to do something like that, but I'm not that brave. I'll stick with my practical brown hair with a few caramel highlights. I also can't help but notice her purple and gold eye makeup framing the longest eyelashes I've ever seen in person. Those things *have* to be fake.

"I loved that movie," her friend gushes. "Definitely one of my favorites."

Ah yes, the "supportive" friend/opportunist whose sole purpose is to help Mikenzie spend her money. And she looks the part too, trying to impress everyone in head-to-toe designer attire. Someone should advise her not to try so hard. Her hair is tinted a pale shade of pink, which I guess is the hip thing to do now? Maybe I *should* do something different with my hair. I suppose I could call my hair stylist and request a popular shade of Easter egg, and she'll know exactly what I mean. Although I might be too old to pull that trend off? I don't think I'm supposed to feel this old at the age of twenty-nine.

"Here you are, Ms. Carson," my co-worker Peyton says, handing her the room keys. She's so good at her job. "And if you need anything, please contact us immediately. Oh, and you know Casey Cooper, right? She was just promoted to be our new director of customer relations."

I smile proudly. I've been here at the Fountain Rose Resort and Spa for three years now. I started working here while getting my degree in hospitality management. Truthfully, I thought it would be years before having this opportunity, so I guess I should be thankful Joelle chose to hook up with our boss. Would it be tacky to send her a thank you note? Probably. I guess I could thank the person who reported them, but they were anonymous.

"New director? What happened to Jojo?" Mikenzie shouts in horror.

Jojo?

Ms. Carson is obviously not as excited about my new job as I am. Not that I'm surprised. Everyone knew she and Joelle were close friends. Really, *really* close friends. Alfie, our head of security, says Joelle and Colton used to party in Mikenzie's room all the time. Of course, no one ever reported it because Colton was our boss, and you don't tell on the boss, right? Well, someone finally did report them. They were caught in a compromising position in a vacant guest room while on the clock.

"Joelle is no longer on staff," I tell her politely. "But I assure you we will continue to provide you with exceptional service."

She gives me an uncertain look and opens her mouth to say something but immediately becomes distracted as another regular guest breezes through the revolving door and into our grand lobby.

"Is that Phoebe Phord?" Mikenzie's friend whispers loudly.

Mikenzie shushes her. We all look at Phoebe, who's carrying two Gucci shopping bags. Phoebe's face is flawless as usual, her skin delicate, like porcelain. She looks amazing for being in her late fifties, not that it's difficult to achieve with the best plastic surgeons and fitness trainers money can buy. I know for a fact you have to pay good money to achieve a complexion like hers.

As she approaches us, I immediately notice that she's wearing the Divine Blessings bracelet I gave her for her birthday. It has Swarovski simulated pearls set in an adjustable handwoven cord. Honestly, I never thought she'd wear it along with her expensive designer jewelry, but I didn't know what else to get her. What do you give a person who already has everything? She gave me a Louis Vuitton wallet for my birthday, but there's no way I could afford to give a gift like that.

Anyway, she started crying when she opened the box. I was really surprised when she told me it was the most thoughtful gift she had ever received and would always wear it. At first, I thought she was just being nice, but she always has it on.

Phoebe rushes toward me, throws her arms around me, and pulls me into a tight hug along with her Gucci bag. "Casey, have I received a package yet today? It's extremely important."

I notice Mikenzie's eyes grow wide as she looks back and forth between Phoebe and me.

"Not that I know of. Peyton?"

Peyton shakes her head as she eyes Phoebe's shopping bags.

"Phoebe, is that you? How are you?" Mikenzie interrupts like they're old friends who haven't seen one another in years.

Phoebe gives her a blank stare, and I try to hide my smile.

"I'm sorry. Have we met?" she asks. "Please forgive me. I have a terrible memory."

Mikenzie tries to hide her annoyance. "Yes, but it's been a while. I'm—" She stops talking and looks around. "Mikenzie Bronsyn. But I'm staying here under my alias. You know better than anyone how relentless the paparazzi can be. They're so obsessed with every move we make."

"Indeed. Well, it's lovely to see you," she says unconvincingly.

Mikenzie smiles smugly, and her friend beams, obviously thrilled about hitting the jackpot in the friend department. If only she knew that Mikenzie is always bringing in random friends, and I don't often see them more than once or twice. She must cycle through them pretty quickly. This very well might be her only chance to be Mikenzie Bronsyn's bestie.

"So, you've met Casey?" Mikenzie continues. "I just heard she's our new director of customer relations. I'm used to working with Jojo, and she was fabulous."

I glance at Peyton, who's placed her hand over her mouth to hide her smile. She's completely amused by the fact that Mikenzie is asking about me while I'm standing here. Not that it's a surprise to any of us. Mikenzie has quite the reputation of having very little tact, and she didn't bother with any staff members other than Joelle. Well, except to bark orders or complain.

"Of course, Casey's like the sister I never had," Phoebe says, putting her arm around me and giving me a squeeze.

Mikenzie purses her lips together.

"She even gave me this very special bracelet for my birthday," she says, holding out her arm. "It's one of the most unique gifts I've ever received, and I never take it off."

I smile. I love that Phoebe thinks of me as a sister because the feeling is mutual. We've known each other for over two years, ever since she became a regular guest and resident of the hotel. We became good friends, but not in a weird way like Joelle's friendships with guests. Phoebe has been there when I've been extremely lonely, particularly during the holiday season. My family doesn't live nearby, except for my half-sister, but we don't have much of a relationship. I think the lack of close family relationships is one of the things that helped me bond with Phoebe.

"Really?" Mikenzie asks, sounding surprised. "Well, maybe we should all go to lunch soon? I would love to catch up with you —and get to know you better, Casey."

"Mmm … perhaps," Phoebe replies, sounding uninterested.

I press my lips together to keep from giggling. She's so good at giving the perfect responses. I'm sure the years of people watching her every move have trained her well.

As if she planned it perfectly, her phone rings from inside her bag.

"I need to get this call," she says, taking her phone out of the bag. "Please let me know when my package arrives. It should be in a large envelope."

"Of course," I reply. "I'll message you as soon as it's delivered."

She cradles the phone on her shoulder. "Thanks, love. I'll be attending an event but not until later tonight. It should arrive before then." She blows a kiss before rushing away.

I know how much Phoebe hates awkward encounters, and this Mikenzie situation would definitely count as one.

"An important package? I wonder what it could be," Mikenzie's friend whispers.

Mikenzie waves her hand, clearly telling her friend to be quiet.

"Well, Casey, if Phoebe endorses you, then I'm sure you will do a fine job," Mikenzie says a few seconds later.

I force a smile.

"And I would really love to do that lunch with Phoebe ... and you. Can you make the arrangements?"

I clear my throat as I try to answer in the most professional and noncommittal way possible. "I will follow up with Phoebe and let you know." *Not bad, Casey.*

"Good. Let's go, Coco," she announces.

Coco? Jojo? Does she give everyone a nickname? *Will I have my own nickname soon? Case? Caso? Maybe I can suggest my own?*

The girls make their way toward the bar.

Peyton throws her head back and lets out a frustrated groan. "Ahhhh. Are you really prepared to deal with that on a regular basis? It's barely lunchtime, and I'm already exhausted," she says, pointing in the direction of our wonderful guests. "We really should do something about her. When are you meeting with the new general manager? What's his name again?"

"Maxwell Sheridan. And he should be here sometime today or tomorrow."

"Maxwell, Maxwell. Sounds very proper. I hope he's not super serious and uptight."

I rub my forehead. "Considering the mess Colton left, I wouldn't be surprised. Apparently, he has a ton of experience running hotels. So just be prepared for a lot of changes around here."

"A ton of experience?" She makes a face. "Do you think he's older? He's probably rigid and strict. Belinda will love him."

I think about our know-it-all co-worker. She would love a manager who's uptight and all business all the time.

I shrug. "I don't know. I didn't ask his age."

"Yeah, that's probably a good thing," she agrees. "Regardless, we need to plead our case to ban Ruby/Mikenzie from staying here. I think she's stolen more than she's paid."

"Probably. But remember, *our guests mean the world to us*," I announce our slogan in my most professional voice.

Peyton makes gagging noises.

"Now, now …"

"I'm only kidding. You know I love our guests," she says, giving me a wink.

"I know you do, with a few exceptions," I say with a giggle. "And don't forget that it's my job to know how to handle situations like Mikenzie Bronsyn."

She rolls her eyes. "Don't you mean *Ruby Carson*? Joelle certainly had her own way of handling her, if you know what I mean."

Of course I know exactly what she means. Joelle's personal relationship with Mikenzie had been hotel gossip for quite a while, long before the news of Joelle's relationship with Colton broke. Their relationship differed drastically from my friendship with Phoebe. Then again, partying and doing drugs with hotel guests was not my style.

"Yeah, I won't be using that alias or Joelle's methods of customer relations."

Peyton frowns. "Come on, Casey. Don't be so serious. Promise me you're still going to have fun with me at work even if this Maxwell guy runs a tight ship."

Before I can answer, a couple with two small children approach the counter, giving me the perfect excuse to leave this conversation.

I make my way to *my* office. I actually have my own office now, even though it used to be Joelle's office, and I've been trying to avoid cleaning it out. Who knows what's lurking around in here?

I sit down in my chair, slowly open one of the cabinets behind my desk, and begin sorting through the items. When I'm done, I breathe a sigh of relief. Nothing but old, outdated room service menus and some training manuals and brochures.

I know for a fact that Joelle used to be good at her job. She was the person who initially trained me, and I remember being in awe of how she handled the day-to-day obstacles with so much patience. She had a way of putting everyone at ease that I wanted to emulate. Things must have changed when she became involved with Colton. This change wasn't a surprise to me because I never thought he was a good manager—that was evident by his behavior.

I don't know anything about Maxwell Sheridan. I just hope he's easy to get along with. Peyton's right though. We still need to have some fun around here. I love working at this hotel, probably a little too much, and I want to keep it that way.

I'm about to open an email when Peyton barges into my office. "Guess what just arrived," Peyton announces waving a thick white envelope in the air. "Phoebe's mysterious package. Where is Mikenzie's friend Coco at a time like this?"

The envelope isn't very large, the size of an average piece of paper.

Peyton holds the envelope up to her ear and shakes it. Her thick blonde curls bounce with every shake. She reminds me of a kid shaking the presents that are under the Christmas tree. "I think it's just a bunch of papers. That seems kind of boring for it to be so important."

I shrug my shoulders. "You never know with Phoebe," I say. "It could be anything—the deed to an English castle, or even samples of some new vegan protein powder."

Peyton makes a face. I know she's hoping for this important package to contain something more exciting.

I hold out my hand to take the package from her. "Regardless, it doesn't matter what it is. I'll let her know it's here." I reach for my phone and text Phoebe then pick up the package and flip it around in my hands. I'm curious too, but like I told Peyton, it's none of my business.

Chapter Two

A few hours after my brief encounter with Mikenzie or Ruby or whoever, Peyton storms into my office for the second time today and folds her arms tightly over her chest. I've managed to clean out two cabinets and solve some guest issues since her last interruption.

"Casey, you need to talk me down because I'm seriously about to lose it. She gets here, and all of a sudden, she's running the show. I don't report to her, so she has no right to give me instructions on how to do my job. I've been working here longer than her anyway."

I can't help but laugh. Peyton only started a month before Belinda. Some people are just not meant to work together, or be in the same room, or breathe the same air. Peyton and Belinda are two of those people. They have a weird, dysfunctional mother-daughter type of relationship. I made the mistake of telling them that one afternoon, and it caused quite a reaction. Peyton didn't speak to me for three days, and I'm pretty sure Belinda tried to have me fired. I have no proof of this, but she seemed very surprised when I showed up for my next shift. Anyway, whatever it is, they can't stand each other.

"You don't have to do what she says. Just ignore her."

She sighs dramatically. "That's what Alfie says too."

"Already talking to Alfie about it, huh?" I tease.

Peyton's cheeks turn a brilliant shade of red.

"You still have Phoebe's package?" She points to the envelope lying on my desk. She's trying to be smooth and divert my attention away from teasing her about Alfie. "For something that was so important, she's not in a rush to get it."

I scratch my head. "I texted her a few times and left a message, but she hasn't responded. Maybe she's preparing for this evening's event?" I send her another text just in case she missed the first few.

Peyton leans in toward me with a wicked gleam in her eyes. "She may be busy. Alfie says her boy toy James has been popping in and out a lot lately."

I shake my head. "I've told you a million times that there's nothing going on between Phoebe and James. Besides, don't you and Alfie have more important things to talk about?"

Alfie is our head of security here at the hotel and my friend. He and Peyton have been flirting for quite a while. Peyton joined the staff after I had been here for two years. Not long after she started, her boyfriend of eight months broke up with her via text. She was an emotional wreck and started asking relationship advice from various guests.

A few months later, he came to the hotel with five dozen roses, begging her to take him back. She did, and that lasted about three months until he hooked up with her uncle's girlfriend at a family party. Anyway, Peyton's relationship history has been public knowledge until Colton told her to keep it outside the workplace. Talk about a hypocrite.

Anyway, I know that's why both she and Alfie are so cautious about their interest in each other. She really has come a long way.

"Casey, you know nothing is as important as our guests," she exclaims, pretending to be appalled at the suggestion.

I laugh. "That's true. If only you really felt that way about all of them."

She pulls her phone out of her pocket. "I guess I better get out there. Belinda says she needs time to call her precious son before I leave. Apparently, he has exciting news for her, *again.*"

We both giggle because Belinda acts like she's mother of the year, but none of us have ever met her son. Supposedly he has some important job that keeps him very busy and always on the go. Judging from comments she's made, you would think he has some kind of top secret government job. She's very vague when we ask specific questions about him but still claims they're best friends. Peyton thinks she's making him up, but I don't think so. I actually feel sorry for her, but only because I have a soft spot for people whose family members blow them off.

Peyton begrudgingly leaves to join her buddy Belinda at the front desk.

A few minutes later, there's another knock at my door. I sigh.

"What is it, Peyton?" I call.

The door opens, and a man pokes his head in. I suck in a bit of air when I notice how attractive he is.

"No Peyton here," he says with a deep voice that echoes against the walls of my small office.

"Oh, um, sorry," I pause as I sit up straight in my chair, "can I help you?"

The stranger opens the door all the way and walks into my office. He's wearing a crisp white tailored shirt under a slate-gray sport coat. I don't see a single wrinkle in his attire or a hair out of place. "I wanted to stop in and introduce myself. I'm Maxwell Sheridan."

He's my new boss. I should have known, judging by his professional demeanor, but admittedly, his good looks threw me for a loop.

I jump to my feet and hurry around my desk to shake his hand. As I approach him, I notice that he's pretty tall, probably about 6'2". And he has very broad shoulders, similar to those of a superhero. Clearly, this man doesn't miss a workout.

"It's nice to meet you, Mr. Sheridan. I'm Casey Cooper. Although I guess you figured that out since you're here, in my office." I'm rambling, but he doesn't seem the least bit phased.

"Yes, I figured you were Casey. And you don't have to call me Mr. Sheridan. Just Max is fine."

Max. He looks like a Max.

My voice jumps to a higher octave. "Great. And I'm Casey."

I sound so juvenile. Why am I so nervous?

"I've heard good things about you, Casey," he replies.

"You have?" Thankfully he doesn't notice I suddenly sound like a high-school cheerleader.

"Your reputation is impressive. I believe I've heard 'organized, efficient, and very dedicated to our guests.'"

I feel my cheeks get hot. "Our guests mean the world to us," I sing.

Kill me now. Did I really just sing our hotel slogan?

Max laughs. "You're funny. Maybe you could write a song to go along with the slogan." He gives me a playful smile, and I feel a sudden jolt shoot through my body.

What the hell was that?

I study Max's face. He has warm hazel eyes and a cleft in his chin. I notice a few wrinkles around his eyes and nose when he smiles. He's *very* handsome, in an over-the-top Hollywood actor kind of way. I admit, he's nothing like I pictured he would be.

Casey, you are treading in dangerous water. I need to remember that I have this new job because Joelle was involved with our *married* hotel manager. In fairness, I have no idea if Max is married or not. Nor should I care. He's my boss.

"Um, I didn't mean to sing actually. Peyton and I sometimes joke about the slogan." *Now that was a good response.*

"Really? That's a shame because I liked the song. It was catchy. We could have something here."

We could have what? Is he still talking about the song? I suck in a bit of air. Is he flirting with me?

"Anyway, I don't want to keep you. I just wanted to introduce myself, you know, making my way around and trying to meet everyone today. I'll officially take over tomorrow. I run a tight hotel. So be prepared for the slave driver to come out."

My eyes grow big. Slave driver? *Great.*

He must notice the panic in my face because he cracks another smile. "I'll see you bright and early tomorrow morning, Casey," he says as he leaves my office.

"I'll be here."

I breathe a sigh of relief when he's gone. Well, that was interesting. I hoped the new manager would be easy to get along with, but I certainly didn't expect *that* kind of interaction. Max is definitely attractive—there's no denying that. However, I refuse to let his good looks distract me. I put all thoughts of Max out of my head and put all my energy into my job. A job I got because Joelle was hooking up with her boss, something I'm not going to do. I take a few cleansing breaths and get to work.

Maybe Peyton was right about Mikenzie Bronsyn ... or Ruby whatever-her-fake-name-is. Am I really ready to deal with her on a regular basis? It's been hours since I saw her this morning, and the requests have already been pouring in.

Somehow, she's managed to call me five times in the last hour with various requests and complaints. She's definitely taking advantage of our impeccable customer service.

My phone rings for the sixth time, and I consider letting it go to my voicemail. Instead, I let out a frustrated sigh and answer the phone. After all, this is what I signed on for.

"Hello, this is Casey," I say in the most annoyingly sweet voice I can manage.

"Hey, hon. I'm so sorry to interrupt you. I just have one more tiny request, and then I'll let you get back to—whatever you're doing."

Hon? A few hours ago, she acted like me taking this job was the worst news she ever heard.

"Would you be able to make a quick run to In-N-Out and grab us a few burgers? You know how it is, sometimes a burger hits the spot."

Is she serious? Since when did I turn into Uber Eats?

"Unfortunately, I won't be able to. I have a very busy afternoon ahead of me. Would you like the number for a food delivery service?"

She doesn't say anything for a few seconds. "Oh, really? It would only take you ten minutes tops." I hear the shock in her voice.

Ten minutes? Try at least an hour between traffic and waiting for food. Maybe Joelle did this, but it's not part of my job description, as far as I'm concerned, and until someone tells me different, it's a pass for me.

She reluctantly takes the number for the delivery service after I decline her request a second time then she hangs up without a goodbye.

It's been a long day, and I'm ready to head home when I notice Phoebe's package still sitting on my desk. I guess it isn't as important as she made it sound. I think about what Peyton said about James. I've actually asked Phoebe if she has more than just a business relationship with James, but she insisted he was just a dedicated assistant, and I believe her. She knows about the rumors, but they never seem to faze her. I'm sure she's used to them by now.

Phoebe told me about meeting James at a gallery opening she attended a few months before I met her. He approached her and told her that his mother had been a huge fan of hers when she was on daytime, and he remembered her religiously watching *Love and Eternity* when he was a child. Apparently, he and Phoebe bonded over losing their mothers and, much like me, not having any family around. He told her that he came to California to pursue a modeling career and he was looking for a job. She hired him on a probationary basis, and she says he's been the best assistant she's ever had.

I shoot her another text, letting her know I'll drop off the package in her room before I leave.

When I enter the lobby, Peyton and Belinda are standing side by side at the front desk, both silent.

"Oh, hello, Casey," Belinda exclaims as soon as she sees me. "How's your day been?"

I sigh, thinking about Mikenzie's endless requests and meeting our attractive new manager. "Long."

She purses her lips as she looks me up and down with a disapproving look. "I can see that. You really should fix your neck scarf. We represent this hotel, and our appearance should be impeccable, as you know."

Seriously? Now she's lecturing me about my appearance. Okay, so maybe Peyton wasn't exaggerating.

Peyton gives me a smug look. I sense an I-told-you-so moment coming later.

I force a fake smile as I study Belinda's appearance. Her hair is pure platinum blonde with curls that frame her face. She thinks she looks like Marilyn Monroe. I only know this because she's made it very well known. Truthfully, other than the short bleach-blonde hair, there is zero resemblance to the famous Hollywood icon.

"Did you girls meet Max?" I ask, ignoring Belinda's comment about my scarf.

"*Maxwell* Sheridan? You mean our new general manager?" she asks raising her eyebrows.

I grit my teeth. She really is a piece of work.

Peyton rolls her eyes.

"Yes. Max Sheridan," I reply knowingly.

"Does he prefer to be called Max? I had no idea you knew him personally."

Okay, so she's going there. That's fine. I can handle Belinda "Wanna-Be" Monroe.

"Just met him for the first time today. I think it's great for the hotel to have some fresh blood. It's time we get back to what we are about."

Belinda actually nods in agreement. "Our guests mean the world to us," she adds proudly. Hearing our slogan reminds me of my earlier performance in front of Max. I shudder as I recall the humiliating moment.

"Exactly. Anyway, I'm leaving for the night. I'll see you bright and early tomorrow." I quickly make my getaway before I receive any more unsolicited instruction on how to do my job.

When I arrive on the twenty-seventh floor, I knock on Phoebe's door a few times but am met with no silence. I figure she must've already left for her event, so I swipe my master key card across the door lock.

I step inside one of our hotel's finest suites, also known as the Golden Ambassador Suite. I don't think any ambassadors have ever stayed here; it's just a fancy name. The Golden Ambassador has two bedrooms, a living room area with a huge balcony, and a stunning view of the Santa Monica mountains.

I have no intention of staying, so I immediately place the package on the table in her entry hall. I'm about to leave when something catches my eye on the living room floor.

I notice Phoebe's vintage Louis Vuitton bag on the floor, its contents spilled out everywhere.

"Phoebe," I call her name. There's no answer. "Phoebe?" I call louder.

I stare at the bag on the floor for a few seconds. She must have been in a hurry and didn't have time to pick it up. I head to retrieve the bag when I look toward the master bedroom. The door is slightly cracked, and I see something shiny on the floor. I'm trying not to overreact, but something doesn't feel right. I inch slowly toward the door and peek inside.

I don't think I could ever be emotionally prepared for what I find. Phoebe is on the floor, dramatically positioned almost like she's posing. She's wearing a stunning gold evening gown, her two Daytime Emmys lying on the floor next to her, and there's a sea of colorful pills strewn everywhere.

I begin to scream for help as I frantically reach into my pocket to get my phone. My hands are trembling, making it extremely difficult for me to dial 9-1-1. I drop to the ground next to her lifeless body and try to find her pulse. And then I see it. The bracelet I gave her is on the floor just a few feet away next to the bed. My heart sinks, and the horror takes over when I realize that I'm too late.

Phoebe Phord is dead.

Chapter Three

I'm now sitting in the empty conference room, waiting for my interrogation to begin. When the police arrived, I told them everything I saw, but now I have to wait to give my statement to the detectives. It was definitely unnerving to have a police officer escort me through the hotel. Thankfully, they were willing to use our service elevators so as not to cause more of a stir.

I put my face in my hands and rub my eyes. Not like this will erase the image of Phoebe's body out of my mind. Every time I close my eyes, I see her on the floor in that beautiful gold gown. And when I think about the bracelet a few feet from her body, the tears well up in my eyes.

What the hell happened in the hours since I saw her? As I sit here in a daze, I overhear someone in the hallway mention suicide. I'm so confused right now. *Suicide?* There's no way.

I'm not even sure how much time has passed because after finding her on the floor, everything is a confusing blur. It seemed like an eternity until a housekeeper heard my horrified screams from the floor below. Alfie finally joined me in the suite after she called for help.

After the police and paramedics arrived, it was pure chaos. I somehow managed to pull myself together long enough to give Alfie instructions for Peyton and Belinda to man the lobby. I reminded him to keep our other guests calm despite the caravan of authorities who have been parading through the hotel. Luckily, because of Phoebe Phord's status, her floor was reserved for high-profile guests, and she was currently the only guest on the twenty-seventh floor.

Poor Phoebe. How could this happen? Why didn't I bring her the package earlier? She told me it was important.

I just can't believe she's gone. All of a sudden, I'm consumed with guilt. I've been a terrible friend recently. I've been so busy focusing on my new job, and we've hardly seen each other except in passing. I could have been a better friend to her.

Phoebe's story was actually a sad one. Underneath the fame, couture, and money was a very lonely woman who'd been through a lot. She told me her whole life story over the last year and a half while I was working the graveyard shifts. She used to wander downstairs in the middle of the night when the lobby wasn't buzzing with other guests and cameras. She claimed to have an unrelenting case of insomnia, but I think she was just looking for someone to talk to.

She told me about growing up and how her dear mother supported her dream of becoming an actress. She got her career start on a soap opera called *Love and Eternity*. Her mother was her best friend and biggest cheerleader, but unfortunately, she passed away before Phoebe received her first Emmy. The way Phoebe spoke about her mother reminded me of my own relationship with my grandmother. She was the only member of my family I've been close to.

Phoebe also told me about her wide array of relationships and about her marriages. She married her first husband, one of the producers of the soap opera she starred in, to help escalate her career; her second husband for money; and finally, her third husband for love. Unfortunately, after only a few years of marriage, she lost her third husband to suicide. I know it totally sounds like a Lifetime movie—I actually think there may be one on the horizon—and now her tragic death will be the perfect ending for the film.

Even though I knew she had been through a lot, I never thought it would be a possibility that she would take her own life. Especially after hearing about her devastation over her third husband's death. It doesn't make sense that she would end her life in the same way.

The door opens again, and this time two men walk in.

I rise to my feet. "Ryan, I'm so glad you're here."

"Hi, Casey."

Ryan is *Detective* Ryan Adams—and my roommate's boyfriend.

"I hope you can tell me what's going on," I plead. "I'm so ready to go home."

He gives me a sympathetic look. "I'm sure you are. I talked to Kendall. She saw the news and is very worried about you."

I sigh. "I'm exhausted. Have you been assigned to this case?"

"I'll be assisting, but this is Detective Cain. He's the lead on this one. He's really good. Not as good as me, of course, but decent," he says with a low, deep laugh.

"Don't listen to this guy," Detective Cain interjects. "I taught him everything he knows."

Detective Cain is quite a bit older than Ryan, with thinning gray hair and a round belly that's about the size of a volleyball.

"Hello," I say. "I'm Casey Cooper."

"Pleasure," he says with a scratchy voice. "Such a shame to hear about Ms. Phord. My wife watched her soap opera religiously for years. She will be deeply saddened by this news."

"Have you been to Phoebe's suite yet?" I ask. "Have you found any clues that would explain what happened?"

"We just came from there. We need to go over the details with you, and then you can go home," Detective Cain says, pulling a notepad out of his pocket.

I feel like I'm living in an episode of *CSI*.

He slowly flips through the pages. "You told the officers that you were in Ms. Phord's room delivering something?"

"Yes. Phoebe stopped by the desk this morning, asking about a package she was supposed to receive today. She said it was very important and to let her know as soon as it arrived. I tried to contact her, that was around one p.m. maybe? I left her messages all day, but she ..." I pause and try to swallow the lump in my throat. "Well, she never came to get it, so I decided to bring it to her room before I headed home. That was around six thirty tonight."

He nods his head slowly. "And where is the package now?"

"In her suite on the entry table. I was dropping it off when I noticed her handbag on the floor in the living room. I went to pick it up, and that's when something shiny in the bedroom caught my eye. It turned out to be the awards, and Phoebe was just lying there like she was on display."

I shiver at the memory.

He puts the tip of the pen to his lip. "Okay. So, you didn't give the package to anyone else or see anyone take it during the commotion?"

Wait, what's he saying?

"No. I left it there. On the table in the entry hall."

He glances at Ryan. For some reason, his expression gives me the chills.

"What's wrong?"

He raises his eyebrows. "The package hasn't been found. Are you sure you left it in her room?"

Does he not believe me?

"Of course I did. I put it down on the table near the door," I reply, my voice beginning to quiver.

"Yes, but you've had quite a shock. Did you see anyone else enter the room?"

I can feel my pulse start to speed up. "The housekeeper came after I started screaming, and then our head of security showed up," I insist, my voice shaking as it gets louder. "Maybe one of them picked it up by accident?"

Detective Cain scribbles something in his notebook.

"I'm sure there's a good explanation," Ryan chimes in. "We still have to get the statements from Alfie and the housekeeper. And also question everyone in the hotel who had contact with Ms. Phord today."

I give him a worried look.

"I don't understand. I left it there."

"Can you think of anything else that stood out to you while you were in her suite?"

I shake my head, and then the bracelet pops into my head.

"Wait. I had given her a bracelet for her birthday. It was on the floor near her body. She told me she never took it off. She even mentioned it earlier when I saw her in the lobby. I noticed it when I went to check for her pulse."

Detective Cain continues to make notes.

"Okay, but it's possible she could have removed it earlier."

I chew on my lip. "Maybe—but I don't think so."

He scribbles as I talk.

"I actually have a question for you," I say, my voice shaking even more. "I overheard someone in the hallway mention a possible suicide?"

The detectives glance at each other. "We don't have anything definitive at this time," Detective Cain says.

That's what I expected he'd say. I feel so overwhelmed as I'm trying to process everything that's happening around me.

"Okay, Ms. Cooper, I think we have everything for now. You're free to go home, but we'll probably have questions for you as we learn more."

I sigh loudly.

"Would you like me to walk you out?" Ryan asks.

"Can you give me a minute? I want to collect myself before I have to face anyone else."

He gives me an understanding nod.

After the detectives leave, I close my eyes and take a deep breath. Phoebe's package is not where I left it. What could be in that envelope that was so important someone would want to take it?

A few minutes later, I feel a hand on my shoulder, which startles me out of my thoughts. I look up to find Max standing over me.

That's just great. My new boss. This couldn't possibly get any worse.

"I guess you weren't expecting something like this to happen when you took this new position," I say as I hang my head, taking a few deep breaths to keep myself from crying.

He clears his throat. "No. I mean, I have had guests pass away in my hotels, but I never found their bodies, so I can't imagine how you must be feeling. Especially considering the … situation."

I know he's referring to Phoebe taking her own life. I'm sure the police have to keep him informed since he's the manager.

I shrug. "I'm not sure how to feel. Phoebe wasn't just a guest; she was my friend, a very dear friend. I've gotten to know her well over the years, and I …" I look down at my hands. If I say another word, I will become a bawling mess.

"I'm sorry for your loss," he says softly. "And even though this may not mean much to you at this moment, you've handled yourself very professionally the last few hours. I heard one of your first inclinations was to make sure the guests were taken care of. The front desk staff has done a great job keeping everyone calm following this tragedy. Not many people would be able to do something like that after this kind of trauma."

I look up and give him a grateful smile. "I appreciate you saying that. It does mean a lot." I take a sip from the water bottle an officer brought me.

"Why don't you go home. I know your work day should have ended hours ago."

I nod. "It did, but I had to wait until the police were done questioning me. It feels like it will never end. I already told them everything I saw, and it wasn't much."

He sits down in the chair next to me. "They have to be thorough." He clears his throat again. "The press is already coming out in droves."

I rub my temples with my fingers. "Of course they are. They

stalked her on a regular basis. Those sharks will have a field day with this news."

"We can handle them," he assures me. "In the meantime, the authorities are trying to locate family members."

I frown. "She didn't have any family. It was just her and her mom, and she passed away years ago. She lost her husband also ..." I trail off and close my eyes as I continue to try to keep myself together. This whole situation is tragic.

"I understand how that feels," he says. "My mom was a single mother. I used to beg her for a brother. I even asked Santa for a brother. I'll never forget the look on her face when Santa waved at her."

I laugh, which makes me feel a tad bit better. "Thanks, I needed to laugh," I tell him.

"I'm glad I could help," he says softly.

In that moment of despair, we lock eyes, causing me to feel that strange jolt shoot through my body once again. I quickly look away.

The door to the conference room opens.

"Casey—oh, sorry," Peyton says as she looks back and forth between Max and me. "Mr. Sheridan, I didn't realize—"

"Call me Max," he interrupts as he rises from his chair. "I'll give you two some time."

Max is gone within seconds, leaving me alone with Peyton and her curious expression.

She looks at me, tears filling her eyes. She wipes the corners with her fingers. "This is so awful. Are you okay?" she asks, her voice shaking.

If I said yes, I would be lying. "I don't know—I think I'm in shock."

She nods. "I can't believe she's gone. We just saw her, and she seemed perfectly fine. I don't think she was acting strange, do you? I just told the police everything I could remember about our conversation. She seemed in a great mood to me."

"I know." I sigh loudly.

Peyton puts her hand on my shoulder. "Do you need anything? When are you going home?"

"I was just getting ready to leave. I just want to soak in a hot bath and go to sleep. Well—if I can sleep."

Chapter Four

As I walk through our grand lobby, I feel like all eyes are on me. Belinda is eyeing me from the front desk. No doubt she's making a mental note about the current state of my appearance. I haven't had a chance to touch up my makeup or fix my scarf in several hours, what with dealing with the death of one of daytime television's most beloved actresses.

"How you holding up?" she asks.

I let out a slow breath. "Honestly, I don't know how I'm still standing. By the way, Max said you and Peyton did amazing handling the fallout today."

She stands up a little straighter, jutting her chin out. "That's why I'm here, to make sure our guests are comfortable and happy. And I would have done a much better job than Joelle. We all know what she was doing to get into that position, now don't we? A flip of the hair and a low-cut shirt are powerful tools."

"Mmm …" I'm not sure how to respond to her. Maybe I'm too tired, but I don't see how she thinks she should have been in Joelle's job, which is now my job, and I hope she's not insinuating that I also slept my way to this promotion. Wait. Does she think she should have gotten the director position? And why is she talking about this right now?

"Leave me alone!" a voice shouts, interrupting our conversation. "Get the hell away from me."

Belinda and I turn around to see Phoebe's assistant, James, push his way through the doors. There are questions coming from every direction, and his face is a bright shade of crimson.

"What was your relationship with Phoebe Phord?"

"Did you know she was going to do it?"

"Is it true that you were using her for her fortune?"

Just when I think James is about to completely lose his cool, Alfie appears out of nowhere and helps him escape the questions and camera flashes.

"How can they treat him like that?" Belinda exclaims. "The poor dear is probably going through so much right now."

I have to agree with her on that. I happily abandon our conversation about Joelle to deal with James and the photographers.

"Hello, James. Are you okay?" I ask. Strangely enough, I barely know him. We've chatted a few times about Phoebe's requests, but nothing on a personal level. At first, I thought he didn't like me. I once asked Phoebe about it, she said he was just

protective of her, and I can understand why. I'm sure when you're famous, you have to be cautious with letting people get too close. As her assistant, he probably had to deal with that constantly.

He looks completely distraught. "Can I speak to you in private, Casey?"

Belinda and Alfie are watching intently.

"Um, sure."

"I'm assuming this has to do with Ms. Phord?" Alfie asks.

James glares at him. "This doesn't concern you."

Alfie folds his arms. "As the head of the security for this hotel, it is my concern."

"Calm down," James demands. "I don't owe you any kind of explanation. The last I checked, you're not a police officer."

"Alfie, it's okay," I say. "We can talk in my office."

Alfie frowns. I'm sure he's feeling helpless after what happened today. It's his job to keep everyone in this hotel safe. Maybe he thinks he's being useful if he's present for our conversation. "Fine. But I'll be right outside your door if you need me, Casey."

"Thanks."

James and Alfie follow me to my office. I guess I'm not going home yet.

I sit down at my desk and feel like I may never get up.

James is frantically scrolling through his phone. Belinda was right about one thing—as Phoebe's assistant, he's definitely dealing with a lot right now.

I can't help but notice how attractive he is. He reminds me of a California surfer boy. He's got sun-kissed blond hair, piercing blue eyes, and a perfect tan.

"Sorry. It's been non-stop all day," he says, putting his phone down on my desk.

I nod. "I totally understand. So, what did you want to talk to me about?"

His phone buzzes and he picks it up again. As soon as he finishes, he puts it down again and rubs his forehead nervously. "I just wanted to know what happened when you went to Phoebe's room. What you saw … or anything." He clears his throat. "I guess I'm just in shock."

I lean back in my chair. "I told the police everything. I went to her suite to deliver something, and I saw her bag spilled out all over the floor. I had a bad feeling, so I went to her bedroom. That's when I saw her. She was on the floor, and she had both her Emmys." I pause and think about the awards. "Do you know why she would've brought her Emmys to the hotel?"

He gets a strange look on his face. "She requested that I bring them to the hotel last week. She didn't say why, and I didn't think to ask because this wasn't the first time. She's taken her awards to events in the past."

Hmm … I guess this could be true. I asked her about the Emmys before, and she brought one to the hotel so I could actually hold it in my hand. It was cool.

"So that was it? You didn't see anything else?" he asks, changing the subject.

I give him a curious look. "James, what exactly are you asking me?"

He looks out the window. "I was just thinking about what was happening in those last few minutes ..."

I can feel the tears creeping into my eyes again. "I don't know. I've been thinking the same thing all day. Phoebe was like family to me."

He nods slowly. "And she felt the same way about you. If she told me once, she told me thousands of times how much she loved your late-night talks. She thought of you as a sister."

I give a weak smile. "I appreciate you telling me that."

Neither of us says anything for about thirty seconds.

"I wish I could tell you more. Except ..." I'm about to tell him about the package missing, but for some reason, I stop myself. I'm not sure what the rules are when it comes to discussing the details, and I certainly don't want to interfere with the investigation.

"What were you going to say?"

I bite my lip. "I was just going to say that I know the police will do everything they can to get the facts."

He frowns. "I suppose they will. In the meantime, I have to start making arrangements."

Crap. I haven't even had a chance to think about that part of it.

"Oh, I guess you would have to. Since you're her assistant and there isn't any family to help. What a tragic, lonely ending to such a wonderful person's life," I say as I dab the corners of my eyes.

"Actually, there is one family member. Her cousin, Raven."

Cousin?

"Oh!" I exclaim. "She never mentioned a cousin. Where does she live? Do you know how to get in touch with her?"

This new bit of information confuses me. Why wouldn't Phoebe have told me about her cousin? One of the subjects we often discussed was our lack of family. I'm sure there's a good reason she left this out, but I can't help but wonder why.

"They didn't speak, but I was able to get in contact with her earlier." He presses his lips into a thin line.

This is interesting. The way Phoebe made it sound, she didn't have anyone else except her mom. Not that it's completely unusual. I have four cousins, and we rarely talk, other than the obligatory birthday wish on Facebook. I wonder what happened between them that would cause Phoebe to not acknowledge her existence.

"What did she—the cousin—say when you told her?"

"She was very upset," he says. "She said to keep her posted about the funeral arrangements and that she will be here no matter what."

I'm sure she will be. The fact is, this long-lost cousin is Phoebe's only relative, and her money has to go somewhere.

"Hmm ... if they didn't have a relationship, then why would

she be so eager to come to her funeral," I pause as I fold my arms, "unless she thinks there's something in it for her?"

James frowns. "I don't think that's it. I often suggested to Phoebe that they try to mend fences. No matter what happened in the past, they were family, and there's nothing more important than that."

Why is he getting so defensive?

"Anyway, I didn't come in here to talk about her cousin. I just wanted to know if you saw anything unusual when you found her. Something that would explain how or why this happened?"

I bite my lip. It's obvious he's overwhelmed, but I don't know what he expects me to tell him. Does he actually believe that she would do this to herself?

"No, I mean—it all happened so fast." I sigh. "You don't think she would have done this to herself, do you? Because I don't."

James looks down at the floor before rising to his feet. "I don't know what to think right now." He lets out a frustrated sigh. "I have a lot to do. Please let me know if you remember anything else."

I nod and grab a sticky note from my desk. I scribble my number on it and hand it to him. "I definitely will. Here's my number. Please let me know if I can help with any of the arrangements."

He takes the paper from me and shoves it into his pocket. "I have everything under control, but thank you."

He's gone a few seconds later, and I sit still behind my desk, trying to absorb our conversation and the events that have transpired over the course of the day. My head spins. It bothers me that James would question whether she killed herself or not. He should know her better than that.

Something just doesn't feel right about any of this.

I know life has been busy lately and Phoebe and I haven't been able to spend as much time together, but I would've known if something was seriously bothering her. I just can't believe that she would ever harm herself.

I put my face in my hands and take a few breaths. *What is going on here? What am I missing? Phoebe wouldn't kill herself. I just know it.* This means something else happened to her. But what? The thought sends a shiver through me.

It's time to go home.

Chapter Five

I feel like I've been run over by a truck. I'm so tired I can barely turn the key to get into my apartment. I finally get the door unlocked, drag myself inside, and drop my bag onto the kitchen table. I open the fridge and grab a bottle of coconut water. Coconut water is my newest health obsession, thanks to Phoebe. You name it, I've tried it. South Beach, keto, juicing, and I've even made up my own called the All the Avocado Plan.

I eat avocado with everything.

This was another thing Phoebe and I would talk about. She would come to me with a new health fad to try, and I was always game. I had complete trust in her when it came to health because she took really good care of herself. This makes me think about those pills I saw on the floor in her room. Phoebe was too health-conscious to take all of that stuff. She was always talking about natural alternatives. I need to tell the detective that. I didn't even think of it until now because I was so exhausted when I was giving my statement.

Considering the day I've had, I probably deserve something stronger than coconut water. *Perhaps a few bottles of wine?* What does one drink after a long day of work? What about a long day of work that includes finding a dead body? And not just any body, but the body of my friend?

I could Google it, but I don't know the rules about Googling dead bodies … and that's probably not the smartest search history to have on your computer.

"Casey, you're finally home," Kendall says, coming out of her room. "Did you see Ryan?"

I kick off my shoes and sit on the couch, pulling my legs tightly to my chest.

"Yeah, I talked to him." I take a sip of my coconut water and wipe away the tears that are once again escaping my eyes. "This has been one of the longest and most difficult days of my life."

Kendall sits down next to me and puts her arm around me. She has a charcoal mask on her face, which is a typical part of her beauty regime. As an aspiring actress, she says her face is her most precious commodity. Personally, I would never use one of those masks, even if I were an actress. I've seen those videos of people ripping the thing off their faces along with the top layer of their skin. The image still makes my skin crawl.

"I just feel terrible. I can't believe my friend is gone. I wish I had been able to help her. I should have gone to her room sooner. Now there are questions about whether or not she took her own life, but I don't believe it for a second. She would never do that. She often talked about the pain it caused those left behind. And she knew it firsthand after losing her husband to suicide."

Kendall raises her eyebrows.

"What?"

She shakes her head like she wants to say something. "I don't know."

"You don't know what? Just say it."

She lets out a huff of air. "This may sound strange, but you know nothing shocks me anymore."

I'm reminded that Kendall does know how I'm feeling. She went through a horrific ordeal of her own after there were several deaths at the movie studio she works at.

"I could just be projecting because of my own experiences. I don't even know her—"

"Kendall," I try interrupting her ramble.

"—and just by the way you described her—"

"Kendall!" I shout louder.

"—maybe she *didn't* do it."

Finally. Someone is thinking along the same lines as me.

This brings up another issue—the thought of someone else killing her and being in our hotel at the same time as the rest of us. It's too much to comprehend. Especially after hearing that the package I delivered is now missing. Was the package connected to her death somehow?

"That's exactly what I've been thinking," I tell her. "What if someone killed her but set it up to look like a suicide?" I close my eyes as I try to process my thoughts.

"I know it sounds insane and I should mind my own business, but look at what happened at Blossom," she says.

"Oh, I know. And it doesn't sound insane at all. There's something else that's been bothering me ..." The bracelet flashes through my mind again.

"What?"

"She always wore this bracelet I gave her for her birthday, but when I found her, it was lying on the floor near her body."

She shrugs. "So, maybe she took it off?"

"Yeah ..." I trail off. "I just think it was odd that it was right there. When I saw her earlier in the day, she mentioned how she never took it off. It almost seemed like it was there for a reason.

"What do you mean?"

"I'm not exactly sure, but what if I was meant to find it ..."

Kendall lightly touches her charcoal mask. "Crap. I have to get this thing off before it's permanently stuck to my skin," she says, quickly standing up. She pauses before heading to the bathroom. "Casey, just be careful. If someone did this to Phoebe, they went out of their way to try to make it look like she killed herself."

The hair stands up on the back of my neck. "I know, and that's truly terrifying."

She nods. "Yes, it is. The thought of someone around you being capable of taking another person's life is—" She shakes her head before rushing off to the bathroom, leaving me alone with my thoughts.

I stretch out on our plush gray couch and hug a throw pillow tightly to my chest. I lie still, listening to the sounds around me: Kendall humming in the bathroom, the humming of the refrigerator.

My eyes begin to close, and Phoebe's body flashes through my mind, immediately causing me to quickly jump to my feet. Every cell in my body is begging me to go to bed, but I need to take a hot shower to relax, and also because I feel disgusting. I really wish it were possible to wash away bad memories too.

I force myself to get off the couch and make my way to my room. I cringe when I see myself in the mirror. My light brown eyes are overshadowed by the puffy, tear-drained swelling. What's left of the morning's eye makeup is now smudged in the corners and under my lash line, and of course my head hurts. Hopefully a hot shower will help.

I take my time in the shower, letting the warm water pour over my head. When I'm finished, I put on my favorite yoga pants and curl up under my soft, white down comforter.

For some reason, James pops into my head, and I think about his question. What did I see in Phoebe's room?

Ugh, I'll never be able to forget. Phoebe in her gold gown with her Emmys next to her. In an odd and twisted way, it seemed like she was on display for the whole world to see her.

I pull the comforter tighter around my body, and I'm about to drift off to sleep when another thought pops into my head.

The scene really was perfectly staged ... *almost too perfect*. She spent her life in the spotlight, drawing attention to herself. Like Kendall said, someone went to a lot of trouble to make an impression. They obviously wanted her to be lying there with the dramatic flair she was known for. It seems like whoever did this knew her and wanted to make a point. That brings me back to the question of who would do this —and why?

I'm jolted from a restless night sleep at six o'clock a.m. I frantically push on the phone screen to shut off one of the sounds that brings ultimate misery—the alarm.

I lie still with my eyes closed as I push back tears—I'm surprised I have any left.

I made the mistake of looking online last night. I saw one article after another tearing into Phoebe's life, all suggesting she took her own life. I have no idea what time I actually drifted off to sleep. All I remember is lying in bed, crying for what felt like hours. My mind spun with all the what-ifs and potential explanations for yesterday's nightmare.

I wish I could call in sick today. I'm sure everyone would understand, given the circumstances, but today is Max's first official day. The last thing I want to do is to give him the idea that I can't handle stressful situations that could arise in my job. Yes, the events of yesterday are rare (I hope!), but I still need to put on a brave face and show why I was given this opportunity.

I roll out of bed and jump into a hot shower. The only thing that distracts me from images of Phoebe is the interaction I had with Max yesterday. It felt like we had a connection. Of course, I could be completely off base and reading too much into it. Yesterday was an emotional day for me, so imagining that I had a moment with my new (and very good-looking) boss is completely possible. I think it's been proven that stressful and traumatic situations bring people together. I even saw Peyton and Belinda being civil to each other. That's never happened before and probably will never happen again. I mean, it took someone dying for it to happen, so in that case, let's hope it doesn't.

I continue to daydream as I mindlessly get ready for work. I add some loose waves to my hair and use half a bottle of concealer to cover the bags under my eyes. I'm not sure why I'm bothering with the eye makeup considering my eyes fill with tears every time I think of Phoebe.

After standing in my closet forever, I decide on a fuchsia blouse to go under my black jacket. I tie a scarf loosely around my neck and smooth down my skirt and take a few cleansing breaths as I mentally prepare for what this day will bring.

When I arrive at the hotel, Peyton is cheerfully talking to a few guests at the front desk. I look around the lobby, and I'm reminded that life goes on regardless of tragedy. People are buzzing around excitedly, ready to enjoy some time at our grand hotel. From what I can see, none of them seem concerned with Phoebe's death. And why would they be? I, on the other hand, need to figure out how to keep it together. I have to work through my grief no matter what it takes.

The press is already painting the picture that Phoebe took her own life. I really should avoid all sources of media, at least for now. It makes me sick to my stomach to think about all the possible ways they could spin this situation. I know it won't be long before the conspiracies start—unless they already have.

Our lobby is definitely my favorite spot in the entire hotel. I've always been in awe of the marble floors, elegant furniture, and exquisite chandelier. Not to mention floor-to-ceiling windows that let in an abundance of natural light. I could totally live in our lobby. When I was younger, I would dream of staying in a place like this, and now I get to come here every day. I feel so grateful for this, even on days like today.

I don't even realize that I'm standing in the middle of the lobby staring off into space until I catch Max watching me curiously from behind the front desk.

Here we go.

His eyes are fixed on me as I make my way toward him. The corner of his mouth turns up into a half smile, causing a stir within me. Whoa, I need to pull myself together.

"Good morning, Casey," he says politely. "How are you feeling today?"

"Morning." I clear my throat. "I'm trying my best to hold it together. I had a difficult night, but I'm here."

I can only imagine what he's dealing with right now. I'm sure he didn't expect such an awful thing to happen when starting his new job. It's definitely not the way I would want to kick off new employment.

"Okay, so far. I would like to have a quick meeting at nine, if you don't mind. I've spoken with Detective Cain, and we have a few important things to discuss. I'll just come to your office."

He seems like a different person from yesterday, so reserved and professional. This must be what he was talking about. The slave driver version of Max is showing his face.

I try to swallow the lump in my throat. "Okay."

He walks off without another word. I watch as he approaches every guest in the lobby. He's very good with the guests, engaging and welcoming them to our amazing hotel. He's probably exactly who we needed here. Colton would rarely come out of his office, and now we all know about the activities he was engaging in behind the scenes.

"How's it going?" I whisper to Peyton. "Max is definitely in full-blown work mode." I wave at an elderly couple as they walk by.

"Oh yeah," she says. "There's some crazy stuff going down right now. Alfie said he couldn't tell me anything yet, but I'm totally freaking out." She turns and greets a man wearing a business suit as he walks by. "Good Morning."

"What do you mean by *crazy*?" I ask. "How can it be any worse than yesterday?"

She shakes her head. "I don't know. I think he's stressing out with the change in management. It *is* his job to keep us all safe."

This reminds me about my conversation with Kendall last night.

"Peyton, I'm having serious doubts that Phoebe did this to herself, and I hate that the press is ripping her name apart," I say under my breath.

"You too?" she replies. "Personally, I don't believe the suicide thing. I think someone killed her."

We look at each other in horror.

"What makes you think that?" I ask eagerly.

She furrows her brow. "I'm not sure exactly. Phoebe was very sure of herself. I just don't see her ending her life in that way." She folds her arms. "Not that people can't put on an act and pretend that everything's fabulous. I still don't think that's the case here."

That's very logical.

"Well, Max just told me we're having a meeting this morning. Hopefully, I'll get some more info. It would be helpful to know what we're dealing with."

A group of five women walk through the door and make their way toward the front desk.

"Welcome to the Fountain Rose Resort and Spa," Peyton says cheerfully.

I glance at their matching T-shirts that say *Meri's Getting Married*. Clever. The girls are giggling and talking about the escapades they have planned for the weekend. I've never taken part in one of those wild bachelorette party weekends, but I've witnessed some of the behaviors working in this industry. It's safe to say it's going to be a busy few days here at the hotel.

I leave Peyton to do her thing and make my way to my office. I sit down at my desk and rub my temples. I knew this was going to be a hard day before I arrived. I just need to do whatever I can to focus on why I'm here. *Focus, Casey, focus.*

I jump right into my job, listening to the voicemails that I missed yesterday while I was dealing with the Phoebe … situation.

"Casey. This is Ruby Carson. I need to book two suites for this coming weekend. I prefer them to be on my floor and adjoining, with a view of the mountains, and keep the complimentary Cristal flowing. Jojo always took care of this stuff, but since you took her job, I'm counting on the same attention and detail."

I roll my eyes while taking notes on her message.

"Casey, Ruby again. Can you inform housekeeping that I expect them at the exact same time every day? If they are early or late, it will interfere with my meditation time."

Meditation? Sure. I delete the message.

"Casey, I haven't heard back from you yet."

Seriously? This message came in two minutes after the previous one.

I'm surprised she hasn't messaged me about Phoebe yet. She's totally the type to lurk so she can find out as much gossip as possible.

I answer a few other guest requests then turn my attention

back to Mikenzie/Ruby. It's my job to keep her happy, whether I like it or not.

There's a knock on the door, and Alfie pops his head in. "Hey, do you have a minute?"

"Sure."

He walks in and closes the door behind him. "I just met with Max, and I know you're having a meeting with him next, but I wanted to check on you first."

I sigh. "I'm here. What did Max have to say?"

He scratches his head. "He wanted to go over which staff members have the most access to different areas around the hotel. And just a heads up—people are talking about you going to Phoebe's suite."

I frown. "Wait. Why would anyone talk about that? I was in there for a reason," I say, raising my voice. I then exhale deeply. I really need to calm down.

"I know that," he says. "They're talking to everyone on the staff. But ... you were the person who found her. The police also questioned me because I arrived in the room a few minutes after you did."

Alfie's phone buzzes and he holds up his hand to stop me. "Damn, I've got to take this. I wasn't trying to worry you. I just wanted to give you an update on what I heard."

He's gone within seconds, leaving me to absorb what he said.

I'm trying to stay as calm as I can, but I'm a wreck inside. Is this what it was like every day of poor Phoebe's life? People telling lies and her having to wonder what others thought about her? No amount of fame or success is worth how I'm feeling at this very moment. I glance at my phone and take a few breaths. It's time for my meeting with Max, and I have no idea what to expect.

Chapter Six

*A*fter my conversation with Alfie, I open my laptop and try to make it look like I'm being productive. I refuse to overreact. I already know people are talking about me, so panicking is the worst thing I can do right now. I need to take a few calming breaths and maybe find a good cup of tea somewhere. My grandma always used to say a good cup of tea can solve any worry. *Sigh.* I really wish that were true, especially right now.

My phone buzzes with a text from my best friend, Jenn.

> SAW THE NEWS. I CAN'T BELIEVE IT. WHY DIDN'T YOU CALL ME?

Jenn met Phoebe a few times while visiting me at the hotel. Phoebe said she reminded her of one of her favorite co-stars, and of course Jenn was on cloud nine after hearing that.

I text her back.

Sorry. It was a crazy day.

A few seconds later, my phone buzzes.

Such sad news about Phoebe. She was a sweet lady. You ok? Sorry about last weekend.

We were supposed to go out last weekend, but once again, she canceled plans on me. I rarely see her these days, being that she's blissfully happy in her relationship. She's been dating Chad for a while now, so her canceling on me is nothing new.

Not that I can blame her. Chad is *any* girl's dream guy, and I'm really happy for her … and not a bit jealous. Well, maybe a tiny bit. I guess this sort of thing happens when you find your soul mate. I wouldn't know since I haven't experienced it yet.

Kendall, Jenn, and I used to be roommates. Jenn moved out about a year ago, shortly after Kendall went through her terrorizing ordeal at Blossom and it followed her home. It was a really stressful time for all of us. Although I'm almost positive Jenn was looking for a good excuse to move in with Chad anyway. When the chaos ensued, she had the perfect reason, and that was it.

My social life changed from that point on—meaning it went from semi-active to almost nonexistent. That's when I really started working even longer hours at the hotel and when Phoebe and I became even closer. This opportunity wouldn't have happened if I hadn't poured my heart and soul into my job. I guess everything happens for a reason. Jenn found the love of her life, and I got my dream job. We both came out as winners in all of this.

I shoot her a response.

> IT'S BEEN QUITE A SHOCK. THINGS ARE WEIRD HERE AT
> THE HOTEL. HOPE WE CAN CATCH UP SOON. I NEED MY
> BEST FRIEND RIGHT NOW.

As soon as I send the message, Max appears in my doorway.

I quickly put my phone down when I see him. Ugh. I'm being so ridiculous.

"Hey. Thanks for meeting me," he says.

I let out a nervous laugh. "Well, considering you're my new boss, I don't think I have another option."

Hmm … I'm not sure where that courage came from.

"Good point," he agrees.

I press my lips together. The curiosity is eating away at me, so I decide to just come out and ask him. "So, does this meeting have something to do with the investigation and me being in Phoebe's suite yesterday? In case you haven't figured out, word gets around quickly in this place."

He raises his eyebrows. "Oh, I've definitely figured that out. And to answer your question, they are investigating deeper into Ms. Phord's death, and although it looks like a suicide, there is some doubt."

"Good, because I have my own doubts as well," I say firmly. "And I'll do whatever it takes to prove it." He raises his eyebrows as I continue talking. "I was in my office until I went to deliver her package." *I feel like I'm constantly repeating this.* "Peyton and Belinda can vouch for me. And so can you. You were in my office when I was singing that stupid song."

His lips turn up into a smile, and I can't help but notice that he has great lips.

What? *Why am I thinking this?* There's something very soothing about his smile though.

"I certainly won't forget that song," he teases.

I throw my hands in the air dramatically. "Exactly."

I actually prefer talking about humiliating myself over discussing the fact that my name is being associated with the death of a beloved actress. Okay, I need to breathe and relax.

Can I call Uber Eats to bring me a cup of tea?

There's a knock on the door, and Detective Cain peeks around the door.

"Come on in," Max says.

I nod my head at Detective Cain because, for some reason, I'm unable to utter a simple hello. He's obviously earned his position because he manages to read my nod and silence without fail.

"Ms. Cooper, I know this seems excessive, but it's our job to ensure we've exhausted all possibilities. You were one of the last people to speak with Ms. Phord, and you found her."

"So, that makes me a person of interest?" I say, raising my voice a few octaves.

"Casey," Max interjects, clearing his throat. "I mean, Ms. Cooper is very concerned about her name being brought up.

As she told you, she and Ms. Phord were very close. On top of everything, she's mourning the loss of a loved one."

I shoot Max a grateful smile, and for some reason, his presence calms my nerves a bit. He said everything I wanted to say without sounding defensive or talking in circles.

Cain nods. "I understand. Keep in mind we're still waiting on the medical reports as well. That will give us a clear indication of the cause of death and timing."

"I have every intention of cooperating with whatever you need," I say firmly. "Phoebe deserves justice, and I don't believe for a second she took her own life. I was thinking about it all night, and I really believe someone did this to her. The way her body was on the floor—it was so perfectly staged."

Detective Cain raises his eyebrows. "Ms. Cooper, I know you said you gave us every bit of information you could remember from yesterday, but are you sure there is nothing else you can think of?"

"Yes, a few things actually. First of all, there were all those pills on the floor. The more I think about that, the more that seems strange. Phoebe was über health-conscious. I can't tell you how many times she talked to me about alternative health options. You could just look at her and see how much she cared about health and fitness."

He nods thoughtfully.

"And I mentioned the bracelet I had given her being on the floor near her. She always had it on, and if she had taken it off, I really believe it would have been in a jewelry box or on a dresser or something. I'm wondering if she wanted me to see it."

He takes out his notepad and starts to scribble.

"Maybe dropping the bracelet on purpose was her way of sending me a message." I glance at Max, who's watching me intently. "It may sound crazy, but …" I stop and try to swallow the lump that's forming in my throat. I push back the tears that are threatening my eyes.

"Nothing sounds crazy to me, Ms. Cooper. And just so you know, we've submitted the bracelet as possible evidence," Detective Cain says.

"That's good."

"Now, I want to review what happened when you talked to her. Can you recount the interactions? Was she wearing the bracelet when you saw her earlier in the day?"

I know I already went through this, but if being thorough helps, then I'll do it.

"Yes, she was definitely wearing it. I noticed it when we were talking. And as far as interaction with her, I told you, she was very clear that the package she was waiting for was important." I pause as I sort through the details in my head.

"It arrived not long after we talked to her, and I sent her a text as soon as it came. I never heard back from her, and that was hours before I went to her room."

"So, you aren't sure what she did after your conversation?"

I shake my head. "She got a phone call and rushed off. I never saw her after that … well … you know."

I never saw her alive.

"Did she say who the call was from, or did you hear her while she was on the phone?"

I frown. "No, but I'm pretty sure she wanted to escape because another guest was there, and she's … um, a handful." I'm careful with my description of Mikenzie. Max is still present, for which I'm grateful, but it's not exactly appropriate to bash guests, whether they deserve it or not.

The detective flips through his notes. "You're referring to Mikenzie Bronsyn?"

"Yes. She claimed she knew Phoebe and then was complaining about me being the new director of customer relations. She was friends with the previous one and had doubts about me taking over. Phoebe vouched for me, and that was enough for her. She then asked to go to lunch with us."

I glance at Max who raises his eyebrows.

I know this information may not be important, but they want every detail, so that's what I'm giving them. "Mikenzie's friend was also there, along with Peyton," I say. "The friend—Coco, I think—was very curious about Phoebe's package."

Detective Cain nods as he makes notes. "So other people knew about the package?"

"Yes. When Phoebe arrived, I was in the middle of a conversation with Mikenzie and her friend. Phoebe interrupted us, asking if it had arrived yet."

"Did Ms. Phord mention this package to you prior to yesterday?"

I shake my head. "I hadn't seen her for several days." I pause. "I was busy with the new job. We'd texted each other a few times, but it wasn't about anything specific."

I look at Max who gives me a small smile. I appreciate his reassurance.

"I'm assuming the package hasn't turned up?" I ask, already knowing the answer.

"Not yet."

"Someone obviously took it. Like I told you yesterday, I set it down on the entry table in her suite, and then I noticed her bag on the floor," I insist.

He flips through his notes and circles something on the paper.

"You said that you and Ms. Phord were very close."

I nod.

"Did she ever mention any enemies or having a falling out with anyone in particular?"

I cup my chin while I think. "Not anyone specifically. I mean, she mentioned people not liking her in general, but I always thought that would be normal for someone like her. She was famous and beautiful and rich."

A thought pops into my head. What if someone killed her because of these reasons?

The detective closes his notepad. "Ms. Cooper, I appreciate your time. I know this is a difficult time for you, and it's hard to relive such tragedy."

I look down at my hands. "Yes, but it's necessary to find out what really happened to her. I knew Phoebe very well, and she wouldn't have done this to herself. Someone must have killed her, and I think that missing package has something to do with it."

Max stands up to walk the detective to the door.

I stay seated at my desk and let out a deep breath.

I pick up my phone and relief washes over me when I see a response from Jenn.

> I'M SO SORRY. OF COURSE. DOES TONIGHT WORK FOR YOU?

"Do you feel a little better after talking to him?" Max asks.

I look up from my phone and shrug. "I'm not sure. I just hope he really listened to my thoughts about someone else doing this to her."

We're both quiet for a few seconds.

"Why don't you take the rest of the day off?" Max says softly. "I think it will do you some good to be away from here."

As wonderful as that sounds, I need to stay busy. Sitting at home isn't going to change anything. I need to be doing things and talking to people. I need to be doing my job.

"I appreciate it, but I would like to stay if that's okay. I'm not sure I want to sit at home alone, and I could use the distraction."

Although, will it really be a distraction? Everywhere I look, I see Phoebe. Not to mention I'm not sure I will be able to go to the twenty-seventh floor anytime soon. I sigh loudly at that thought.

Max gives me a concerned look. "I understand, but I'm not sure this is the place for you to be today. Can you go see a friend or family member?"

I shake my head. "I don't have any family close by, and my roommate has been working long hours lately. I have plans with my best friend, but not until tonight."

Max purses his lips. "Fair enough, but if things get too intense, just shoot me a message and leave."

I feel tears prick my eyes, and I quickly wipe them away. "Thanks, Max."

He looks like he's about to say something but closes his mouth. We both stand up, and I take a few cleansing breaths before I head out to face whatever is waiting for me.

Chapter Seven

"*R*eally, Peyton, the way you speak to some of our guests is deplorable," Belinda says in a loud whisper. "Yours is one of the first faces they see when they come here, and it should exude utter joy that they are here. You should be warm and welcoming."

"I am warm and welcoming," Peyton snaps under her breath. "And I don't care what you think. I don't answer to you."

After my conversation with Max, I walk out of my office and into a typical disagreement between Peyton and Belinda. I'm really not in the mood for their behavior today. Honestly, after what just happened yesterday, you would think they could be civil.

"Can you two stop?" I ask.

They both turn and stare at me.

"We just lost Phoebe. And we have a new general manager. I

would hope you two could put your differences aside while we figure all of this out."

Peyton hangs her head, while Belinda remains stoic and starts it up with me. "Casey, while it is tragic what happened to Phoebe, we still have a hotel full of other guests to take care of." She pauses and waves at two women who are holding tennis rackets. "Do you suggest we abandon our responsibilities even though the situation is out of our hands?"

I fold my arms against my chest. "Of course not, but don't you think the guests can sense your dislike for one another? You certainly don't try to hide it."

Belinda pats her platinum blonde hair. "It's not in my job description to cater to my spoiled and entitled co-workers," she says, giving Peyton the side-eye.

Peyton glares at her.

"And furthermore, I would think that you, as our director of customer relations, would agree with me. I understand Phoebe was your … friend, but you still have an important responsibility."

Peyton gives me an *I-told-you-so* look.

I think for a few seconds about how I should respond to Belinda. I could jump to the defensive, but that won't accomplish anything. So I ignore her comment and address the situation. "You and Peyton need to learn to coexist while here in front of our guests. I doubt Max will tolerate what I just witnessed between you two."

Belinda frowns, and Peyton remains silent.

I've said all I need to and turn to head back to my office.

"Casey, I'm so glad you're here," Mikenzie says as she rushes toward me. Before I have a chance to realize what's happening, she throws her arms around me and begins to sob on my shoulder. "Our poor Phoebe," she wails.

I glance at Peyton, whose jaw is now on the floor.

My arms are still glued to my sides while Mikenzie continues to carry on with the dramatics. And to give her credit, she's very convincing. "I've been in shock since I heard the news." Her arms are still tightly around me. "You must be beside yourself. Now I understand why you didn't answer my messages. I'm sure you're dealing with a lot. Especially finding her like that." She pulls away and places her hand on my shoulder.

"Yes, it's been overwhelming."

Mikenzie begins fanning her face with her other hand, and now I notice a few other guests watching her.

"Ruby, can I help you with something?" Belinda interjects.

Mikenzie barely gives her a side glance. "No, thank you. I would like to speak to Casey."

I look at Belinda, who scowls.

And just like that, I zap back into work mode. No doubt Belinda is judging my every move—maybe she's even taking notes?

"Mikenzie, why don't we move this conversation away from the lobby. I'm sure you can understand that we're trying to keep things as normal as possible here."

She nods in agreement. "Of course, I know better than anyone. I'm so used to being stalked by the media."

I do an internal eyeroll. "I'm sure you do."

I lead Mikenzie to my office. As expected, she enters and sits down in one of the chairs across from my desk. I would rather be doing anything else right now, but suddenly a thought pops into my head. Now is my chance to find out if Mikenzie happened to see or hear anything.

I sit down at my desk.

She dabs the corners of her eyes.

I have to admit, I'm impressed with her display of emotion. I go back and forth between crying and feeling completely numb, but she's carrying on like Phoebe was her best friend.

"Can I get you something?"

She shakes her head. "Not right now. I just need to get this out. My therapist says it's very important for me to release all my emotions while I'm feeling them."

I nod and fold my hands on the desk.

"You seem to be handling this so well," she says. "I would think you'd be a wreck, considering you and Phoebe were so close."

I bite my lip. "Well, I cried all night long. Right now, I'm trying my best to hold it together for work. Truthfully, I don't know what to think or feel right now. It's just so confusing because everything seemed fine during our conversation in the lobby."

She shakes her head as she dabs the corners of her eyes again. I notice that her abundance of tears have suddenly dried up. She really is quite the actress. "I've heard rumors that the police are now thinking she didn't commit suicide. Now there is talk about someone killing her, but that's just not possible."

I give her a curious look. "Why do you say that?"

"A murder? Here in this hotel? No way," she insists. "One of the reasons I stay here is because of the security and safety."

"Well, I'm glad you feel safe here."

She sighs. "I do. And the truth is, everyone in our industry has skeletons, including Phoebe. They obviously became too much for her to handle, and I told the detective that."

I stare blankly at Mikenzie. While it may be true that everyone has skeletons, I knew Phoebe, and my gut tells me she wouldn't have done this to herself.

"Okay, well I'm sure the authorities will find the answers they need," I say, standing up. Hopefully, she takes the hint that I'm done with this conversation. "On another note, I did receive all your requests. I've spoken to housekeeping, and they will do their best to not disturb your meditation."

"Good." She makes her way toward the door but stops. "Phoebe was right. You seem to be doing well in this position, at least so far."

I force a smile.

A few seconds later, she's gone.

I lean back in my chair and stare at the ceiling. This is all wrong, and I don't care what Mikenzie says. The only thing she said that made sense is that we do have great security in this hotel, which means the person who killed her could've already been inside the hotel.

I grab my phone from my bag and text Kendall.

CAN YOU ASK RYAN TO CALL ME? THANKS.

I open my emails and notice a few from Max. New programs, incentives, updated security …

That gives me an idea. I jump up from my desk and head to Alfie's office.

Chapter Eight

"The police took the footage from the twenty-seventh floor," Alfie says, holding his hands up. "That was one of the first things they did."

"Did you look at it?"

"Of course I did," he says defensively.

"Was there anything suspicious on the footage?"

He shakes his head. "No. There was nothing at all."

"You mean there was nothing from the Ambassador Suite? What about other areas? Elevators, the stairwell, hallways ..."

He frowns. "It was all completely blank. We're thinking there was some kind of malfunction. The system is pretty dated."

"Wait, you mean there was no footage from anywhere in the entire hotel?"

"Casey what's with all the questions?" he asks curiously. "You know the police are already on top of this."

"I know." I pause as I feel the tears finally threaten my eyes again. "But I feel like I have to do something. I don't believe Phoebe committed suicide."

He raises his eyebrows. "Okay."

"I was hoping there might be some record of who was on her floor throughout the day. I can't believe the whole system crashed."

He holds up his hands and shakes his head. "I don't get it either," he says. "And the police asked me about that package. I'm as baffled by that as you are."

"Do you remember seeing it on the table when you came in?"

He shakes his head. "Honestly, I didn't notice. Those few minutes were so chaotic. I told the detective that when he asked about it."

I frown. "Do you think she was murdered? Don't you think someone could have set it up to look like a suicide?"

He shakes his head. "Honestly, I think she was a lonely, rich woman who had a lot of issues. Why would someone want to kill her?"

"That's exactly what I want to find out," I cry. "I just feel it in my gut that she wouldn't do this—" I'm interrupted by Alfie's phone ringing.

"This is Alfie," he answers.

I completely zone out while he's on the phone. My brain starts swirling with possibilities. Detective Cain asked if Phoebe had any enemies, and as far as I know, she didn't. She'd been retired from daytime TV for several years and had chosen to live a quiet life doing charity work and traveling. With this in mind, I can only think of one reason that someone would want to kill Phoebe.

Money.

This brings up another thought. What if James is actually involved with her death? He has more access to her life and her money than anyone else. Ugh, the thought makes me sick to my stomach.

"Sorry about that," Alfie says after he hangs up.

"What if it was James?" I blurt out. "He had access to everything in her life. He could have set it all up—the Emmys, the pills, everything. He could've come in and out of the hotel, and no one would have given it a second thought."

This also reminds me of the conversation I had with James. Maybe he was fishing for information when he asked me what I saw when I found her. And he was very defensive when I mentioned her money and the possibility of the long-lost cousin wanting a piece of it. Or maybe *he* wants all that money.

Alfie looks confused. "Yeah, I guess there could be a chance. Just remember they haven't ruled out a suicide yet. I know you want answers, but these investigations take time."

I sigh. "I know, you're right." I drop my face into my hands. "I just want to help in any way I can."

I feel Alfie's hand on my shoulder. "I know this is especially difficult for you. You just have to trust that the police are doing everything they can to resolve this."

I'm suddenly unable to speak because of the huge lump of emotion that's returned to my throat.

He continues, "And I'm sure it's much easier to blame someone for her death rather than consider the alternative ... that maybe you didn't know her as well as you thought."

I look up at him. "You really don't believe someone killed her, do you?"

He shakes his head. "I'm sorry, Casey. It just doesn't make sense."

I tighten my jaw. "Well, the police think it's possible."

"That's not surprising. It's their job to consider every possibility," he replies knowingly.

I sigh and rise to my feet. "Anyway, thanks for talking to me. Promise me you'll tell me if you find or hear of anything else?"

"Yes, definitely."

I give him a grateful smile.

I don't care what he says. I know Phoebe did not kill herself, and it looks like it's up to me to prove it.

"This is madness," Jenn says, scooping some guacamole onto a tortilla chip. "You really don't believe she did it?"

"No, I don't," I say firmly. "Jenn, you don't understand. I can't tell you how many conversations we had about her husband's death and how it affected her. And the way she was lying—" I shiver at the memory.

I wrap a blanket tightly around my lap. Jenn brought Mexican food over, but I still don't have much of an appetite. "And what about the package that disappeared?"

She shrugs. "Maybe a housekeeper took it, or what about her assistant?"

"Yeah, the more I think about all of this, I'm convinced James knows more than he's letting on," I tell her. "And all of a sudden, she has a cousin. I swear she told me she didn't have any family."

"Maybe she didn't think of this cousin as *family*," Jenn suggests. "I have plenty of family members I'd rather not claim."

She has a point.

"Just be careful," she begs. "If there's anything we learned from what happened to Kendall, it's to watch our backs because you never know what can happen."

My heart sinks at the thought.

"I know you want the truth to come out," she continues, "but what if you're right and someone *did* kill her? Their intention obviously was to make it look like a suicide. They aren't going to like you poking around trying to prove otherwise."

I groan and lean my head against the back of the couch. What am I supposed to do? I know Jenn and Alfie mean well, and they're right about letting the police handle it, but there is that part of me that feels I need to do this for Phoebe.

Jenn puts her hand on my shoulder. "Hey, how about I stay here with you for a few days?"

I feel the tears fill my eyes. "You don't have to do that."

She shakes her head. "I know I don't, but I want to. That's what friends are for."

A tear escapes my eye, and I quickly wipe it away.

Even though I told Jenn she didn't have to stay, I couldn't be happier that she is. Maybe, deep down, I want to find out what happened to Phoebe so I don't have to face the fact that she's really gone. And right at this moment, at least I don't feel as lonely as I did.

Chapter Nine

I'm startled by a knock on my office door. This has been happening a lot in the four days since Phoebe's death. As if finding a dead body wasn't enough, add in the fact that I've been living on minimal sleep and coffee and I'm definitely on edge.

"Yes?"

Belinda opens the door and frowns at me.

"What's wrong?" I ask.

"Do you really think it's good for you to be here right now? You're probably not in any condition to deal with our guests."

I admit I've spent most of the day hiding in my office, but I need to be working. I don't want to sit home alone and think about everything that's happening around me. I've done a minimal amount, reached out to several guests, and handled a few housekeeping complaints. Who would have thought guests would actually complain about the toilet paper roll being in the wrong direction? I've heard some outlandish complaints, but this tops the list.

Thankfully Mikenzie has been gone for a few days. Although, she has scheduled a new reservation next week.

"I appreciate your concern, but I've actually been communicating with guests all day."

She folds her arms in such an authoritative way, and for a second, I feel like I'm back in Ms. Hull's seventh-grade geography class. She was such a scary teacher. "Well, there's someone out front who would like to speak to you, and I think she would like to do so in person."

It's time for me to get out and face the world anyway.

"I'll be happy to," I say as I rise to my feet. "Did you ask her what it's in reference to?"

"Of course I did," she replies with an edge in her voice. "She said it was a personal matter, so I didn't pry."

I make my way into the lobby where I see a tall woman typing rapidly on her phone. She has shoulder-length dirty-blonde hair and long pink and white acrylic nails. She's wearing a short denim skirt, an off-the-shoulder sweater, and an entire bottle of perfume.

"Hello, I'm Casey Cooper."

She drops her phone into her bag. "Thanks for meeting me," she says. Her voice is raspy and sultry. She really should have a job on the radio. "I'm Raven Fransen, Phoebe Phord's cousin."

My mouth drops open, and I freeze.

She really does exist. This is Phoebe's long-lost cousin.

"Ms. Cooper?"

I shake my head when I realize I've been staring at her. I'm sure I look super creepy.

"Yes, sorry," I blurt out. "I just—forgive me. Phoebe always told me she didn't have any family other than her mother."

I notice her jaw tighten. "That's not surprising. We weren't exactly close."

Okay, so at least she's admitting it. I want to know more though, so I invite Raven to come to my office. Belinda is watching me intently and motions for me to fix my neck scarf.

I make a mental note to talk to Max about getting rid of these stupid scarves. They were a uniform requirement Colton wanted anyway.

A few minutes later, Raven confidently sits down across from my desk.

"Can I get you something to drink?" I ask.

"How about a martini?"

I raise my eyebrows.

"I'm only kidding. Water is fine."

She totally isn't kidding.

"So, why did you want to speak to me?" I ask.

She runs her hands back and forth on her skirt.

"When Phoebe's assistant contacted me about her death, he told me you were one of the few friends Phoebe had." She clears her throat. "I guess I wanted to meet you.

"Oh, yes. Phoebe was a very dear friend."

She looks away. "Phoebe and I were never close because our mothers didn't get along," she says, taking a sip of her water bottle. "I always wanted a relationship with her, but Scarlett, Phoebe's mother, wouldn't allow it. She was a vicious woman."

Vicious? This sounds nothing like the wonderful, loving woman Phoebe described. "Really? Phoebe always spoke very highly of her mother."

Raven frowns. "I don't doubt that for a second. She was a neurotic, controlling stage mother, and in her eyes, no one else was good enough to associate with Phoebe. Not even her own flesh and blood."

Well, I guess this explains why Phoebe never mentioned her cousin.

"Why didn't your mothers get along?"

Raven purses her lips, and I finally see the family resemblance.

"My mother didn't like to talk about it," she says. "After both of them passed away, I reached out to Phoebe. She was cordial, but she still didn't want to have a relationship with me. She worshipped Scarlett. I guess she didn't want to go against her wishes, even after her death."

I'm completely enthralled in her story. It's actually very sad. When Phoebe and I discussed our feelings about having no family, I really could empathize with how she felt. I can remember one occasion where she told me that her mother often said that people in the world would be out to use her for her fame and fortune. That was another reason she was cautious about getting close to people.

"I was very sad to hear about her death. Although, I am grateful her assistant contacted me. It was better to hear from someone who was close to her instead of the media. I just wished I'd had a chance to get to know the person she really was. I secretly watched her on *Love and Eternity*. My mother would've killed me if she'd known."

A part of me feels sorry for Raven that she didn't get to know Phoebe. But there's also a part of me that's very skeptical of her. Maybe it's the timing, but the fact that she showed up now bugs me.

"So, where do you live?" I ask.

"I live up north. I told her assistant I would come down as soon as I could. Thankfully, I was able to take some time off work."

I furrow my brow. "I'm still waiting to hear from him about funeral arrangements."

She raises her eyebrows. "You're attending the funeral? I was told it was supposed to be a very small guest list."

Obviously, she doesn't realize how close Phoebe and I were. I fight back the urge to cry. I quickly clear my throat. "Phoebe was a really great friend. I'm lucky to have had her in my life."

Raven chews on her lip, and I notice a hint of annoyance in her expression. It's possible that it bothers her that Phoebe was close to me while she didn't want a relationship with her. That's not my fault, but I'm sure it stings.

"Anyway," Raven says with a wave of her hand, "when I spoke to him again last night to tell him I was definitely coming, he said he was finalizing everything. I think he has a lot on his plate right now."

I'm sure he does.

"Where are you staying while you're here?"

She shrugs. "I'll find some place nearby."

Suddenly I get an idea. "Why don't you stay here for a few days?"

She snorts. "I don't think so. No offense, but I think your rates are a bit too high for my budget. Obviously, Phoebe could afford to stay here whenever she wanted."

Hmm … it's interesting that she would mention Phoebe's financial situation. Now I really don't believe it's a coincidence that she showed up after Phoebe's gone. Her money is still here.

"You're Phoebe's cousin. We can certainly comp a few days for you."

Although I'm suspicious of this woman, she is Phoebe's only family member, so I'm sure Max won't have an issue with us accommodating her. It could also give me a chance to learn more about this stranger.

A shocked expression spreads across her face. "That's nice of you. I'll let you know if I don't find anything else."

I try to hide my surprise that she doesn't immediately take me up on my offer.

After Raven leaves, I head to Max's office to discuss my offer to let Raven stay at the hotel. Truthfully, it's a good excuse to see him again.

～

I sit down on the edge of the huge leather chair across from Max's desk. He's on the phone but waved for me to come in when I showed up. I do appreciate the fact that his door is wide open. It's much more welcoming than when Colton was our manager. Of course, his door was closed for other reasons, but whatever.

"How's it going?" he asks as soon as he hangs up.

I immediately tell him about offering to comp Raven's stay.

"Yes, of course, it's the least we can do for a family member. And if anyone else comes, instruct the front desk staff to do the same."

I breathe a sigh of relief because I did that off the cuff. Even though it's my job to handle customers, I haven't exactly had a chance to get familiar with working with Max and his policies. Not that he's had time to make a bunch of changes yet.

"She said she'd let me know if she didn't find another place to stay," I tell him. "I'm glad I didn't assume too much. We haven't discussed your new policies yet. I'm sure you want to make changes around here."

"I have a long list of things I want to update," he says. "Unfortunately, with everything going on, we're moving slower than I would like."

I begin to fiddle with my scarf, which reminds me. "Speaking of changes, can we get rid of these?" I say, pointing to the noose around my neck.

He cocks his head to the side. "You don't like the scarf? I think it's very professional."

Ugh. It's not just the scarf. It's also Belinda and her power trip.

"Honestly, I don't love them. But they also add to a staff issue that's been going on at the front desk."

"A staff issue? Because of the scarves?" He tries to hide his smile.

Crap. That does sound really juvenile.

I shrug. "Sort of, but mostly it's due to a lot of strong personalities."

"Ah, I understand now. My advice to you is to find ways those personalities can complement each other so everyone can work together. You'd be surprised how a few subtle changes can make a big difference."

"Okay. And the scarves?" I ask, pointing at my neck.

He smiles. "I think they look nice."

Okay, I guess the scarves are staying.

"I better get back to work. Thanks for understanding about Phoebe's cousin."

"No problem."

We both stand up at the same time, and he joins me in front of his desk. Our sudden close proximity causes a stir inside me, and for some reason, I don't move. I don't want to move because I feel safe being around him. Ugh! *Do something, Casey!*

"Okay, well, let me know when you want to implement your changes. I think it will be good. The Fountain Rose needs a fresh start. There's been too much negative publicity and ..." I pause as the image of Phoebe on the floor of her suite flashes through my mind.

Max puts his hands in his pockets. "I think the changes will be good for everyone. I'm confident that things will get better around here."

I thank him for his time and head back to my office.

I hope he's right.

Chapter Ten

"*I* can't believe her cousin showed up," Peyton says as she walks around fixing the pillows on the couches in the lobby. "What was she like? Did she tell you why she and Phoebe didn't talk?"

I smile at a few guests walking through the lobby then begin to straighten out the books on the end tables.

"Yes, apparently it had something to do with a feud between their mothers. They weren't allowed to have any communication with each other." I pause and adjust my scarf. "Anyway, I offered to let her stay here, but she declined. If she changes her mind, Max says we should make sure to take care of anything she needs."

"He's turned out to be pretty nice so far, don't you think?" she asks, giving me a coy smile.

"Definitely, especially with what happened the day he arrived."

Peyton frowns.

"What?" I ask.

"He arrived the day Phoebe died, right?"

"Yeah."

"That's an interesting coincidence."

I give her a curious look. Is she actually suggesting that Max could be tied to Phoebe?

"I know it's kind of out there, but stranger things have happened," she says pointedly.

It is a coincidence, but Max came to my office and spent the day touring the hotel and meeting the staff, so I don't see how it could be possible for him to kill and stage a whole suicide scene. No matter what, James is still the number one suspect in my mind. It really is a strange feeling to wonder if someone you've had conversations with could be capable of killing another person. I know it happens every day, but it's still surreal.

"I understand what you're saying, but I don't know of any connection between Phoebe and Max. Not to mention he was around here most of the day. I think the most obvious person would be James, but maybe that's *too* obvious."

"Yeah, you're probably right. Max spent a good amount of time at the front desk. He went to your office too, right?"

I think about my awkward singing moment with Max which makes me cringe.

"Do you remember seeing James come in the hotel that day?" I ask.

Peyton shakes her head. "I don't. It was really busy at the desk, and he comes in and out so frequently, I wouldn't have paid any attention to him."

I sigh. "As far as I'm concerned, she didn't kill herself. Now, I'm just waiting for the official word."

Our conversation is interrupted by a woman wearing at least a pound of diamonds around her neck. While Peyton takes care of her, I hear my phone buzzing in my pocket. As soon as I look at the screen, I see it's a text message from a number I don't recognize.

> HI, CASEY. WE WILL BE HAVING A PRIVATE MEMORIAL SERVICE FOR PHOEBE ON MONDAY. PLEASE KEEP THIS QUIET. I KNOW IT'S SHORT NOTICE, BUT WE WANT TO KEEP THIS AS SMALL AND INCONSPICUOUS AS POSSIBLE. I WILL ATTACH DETAILS. THANKS. JAMES

That's only two days from now.

As I read the details, a huge lump forms in my throat. She will be buried alongside her beloved mother, Scarlett Fransen.

I think about what Raven said about Phoebe's mother. Unfortunately, neither Phoebe or her mother are here to shed any light on what really happened in that family. Raven is now the only one who can confirm anything, and I have no way of knowing if she can be trusted.

~

I'm woken by the sound of my phone ringing. I think the lack of sleep is finally catching up to me. I purposely left my phone on the other side of my room which forces me to get up. Jenn has been staying with me for the last two nights, and I couldn't be more thankful since Kendall has been filming late at the studio.

I finally have a day off today, which also happens to be the day of Phoebe's memorial service. Unfortunately, what was supposed to be a quiet event was somehow leaked, and both Peyton and Belinda were upset they weren't included on the guest list. Honestly, you would think this was a big fancy gala or something.

The truth is that Phoebe really didn't have much interaction with either of them. She usually came to me if she needed something at the hotel, and if I wasn't available, James would handle it.

I have two missed calls from the hotel and a text from Peyton asking me to call her. I roll my eyes because I'm sure she wants to complain about not being able to attend.

"Thank you for calling the Fountain Rose Resort where our guests mean the world to us. This is Peyton."

"It's my day off. What's up?" I say.

"Oh yes. Have you visited our website? Our property is exquisite."

Obviously she can't talk.

"Is Belinda there or Max?"

"Oh yes and yes," she sings.

"Okay, is it an emergency, or did you just want to complain?" I ask.

"We have *two* very luxurious swimming pools."

That's her way of telling me that it's both an emergency and a complaint.

"Can I place you on a brief hold? Thank you."

After five minutes, I'm about to hang up when Peyton picks up the phone.

"This is ridiculous. Mikenzie can attend the funeral, but I can't? Phoebe didn't even know who she was."

Mikenzie?

"Whoa. What are you talking about?"

"She was here at the desk this morning, arranging for a car. She asked for you, of course."

What the hell? James said it would be a private and small gathering. How did she manage to get her name on the list?

"I'm as surprised as you are," I exclaim.

I listen to her rant before she hurries off the phone when Belinda returns. I sit still for a few minutes while I mentally prepare to say a final goodbye to my friend.

I take my time getting ready, starting with a hot bath. This is something I rarely do. I put on my only black dress that doesn't scream "cocktail party," although I know Phoebe would prefer the cocktail dress. The last funeral I attended was my grandfather's about five years ago. I had only met him a few times since he wasn't on the best of terms with my father. That was also the last time my family was all together.

My father remarried and started his life over as soon as my parents' divorce was final. He and his new wife had my sister, Jacy, and they live as one big happy family, complete with a white picket fence, a dog, and a cat.

My mother lives in the Bahamas with her boyfriend, so I don't see her very often either. As soon as I became an adult, my parents were completely off the hook and ready to live their own lives. Over time, I guess I became jaded when it came to family. This has also caused me to become somewhat unemotional regarding relationships. I definitely think I put up a wall a long time ago. That's another reason I loved talking to Phoebe. She felt like family, without all the complications and expectations.

Last Thanksgiving, I was feeling extra sorry for myself. Phoebe spent most of the evening with me in the lobby. My dad and his family were celebrating in Cabo, and I didn't receive an invitation. I had been invited to celebrate with Jenn's family, but it was just easier to go to work. Phoebe listened to me while I had my pity party that night. I told her about how my parents and I would share a pumpkin pie every Thanksgiving when I was younger. We would eat it right out of the pie dish.

The next morning, there was a gourmet pumpkin pie waiting for me at the hotel. This is just an example of one of the thoughtful things Phoebe did for me.

While taking my trip down memory lane, I add soft waves to my hair and apply waterproof mascara to my lashes. Jenn offered to come with me, but I declined because it was supposed to be a private event. I take a few deep breaths and grab my handbag. I have no idea what to expect at this funeral. Hopefully, it's a lovely tribute to my friend—without any drama.

Chapter Eleven

I've never been to the funeral of someone famous so I'm not sure what to expect. Admittedly, I wondered if there would be trays of champagne and maybe some hors d'oeuvres. The idea is not completely unfounded. I've seen some wild things go down at the hotel, and people handle death and grief in different ways. So far, it doesn't seem different from other funerals I've attended, only much smaller. For someone who had many adoring fans, this funeral feels empty.

I immediately notice James speaking to the pastor and a short, round man in a tuxedo. Okay, so I don't think I've ever seen anyone wear a tuxedo to a funeral, but it's not my place to judge. Many people consider funerals to be a celebration of life. So why not wear black tie? I kind of think Phoebe would've wanted it that way.

Raven is sitting in the front row with her arms folded and her eyes closed. Either she's praying or sleeping, I can't be sure. I count eight guests so far, including the pastor. James definitely meant what he said about it being a small group, but how Mikenzie made it on the list is still a big mystery to me.

I slowly make my way down the aisle, toward the front of the church. I approach the gorgeous white casket and pause a few feet away from it. Thankfully, it's closed.

There's a poster-sized picture of Phoebe next to the casket. As I stare at it, I'm reminded how beautiful she was, and this brings tears to my eyes. Just the thought that someone could have taken her life feels like a punch deep in my gut. I continue to mill around in the aisle until Raven calls my name.

"Hey, Casey, come sit over here."

I give her a nod and take a seat to the left of her.

"How are you doing today?" she whispers.

I let out a slow, deep breath. "As good as expected, I guess. I still can't believe I'm here."

Her face falls. "I know the feeling. I was just sitting here thinking about all the years that were wasted. I wanted to have a relationship with Phoebe so badly, but she continued to shut me out over and over again."

Is she trying to make me feel sorry for her? I glance up at Phoebe's picture. "You never called me about staying at the hotel. I'm assuming you found something."

She nods. "Yes. I appreciate your offer, but I'm fine."

Our conversation is interrupted by the sound of painful sobbing. We both turn around to see the sounds are coming from Mikenzie. She's walking down the aisle toward us, her arm linked with a girl I don't recognize and a single red rose in her other hand.

Raven and I watch as she approaches the casket and gently places the rose on top of it. I know I've said it before, but this girl deserves an award for her dramatic skills. I don't doubt she's sad like the rest of us, but she's taking her grief way too far.

"Casey, love, hi," she says, holding her arms out toward me. I plaster a fake smile across my face as I stand. She throws her arms tightly around me while I pat her on the back a few times.

When she finally lets go of me, I motion to Raven. "This is Phoebe's cousin, Raven Fransen."

Mikenzie puts her hand to her chest and tightens her lips. "Oh, Raven, I'm so sorry for your loss. I'm Ruby Carson. We all loved Phoebe like she was our own family. We were all so lucky to have her."

I internally roll my eyes. This isn't the place for me to show my true feelings about Mikenzie and her dramatics.

I glance at Raven, who doesn't appear impressed with Mikenzie at all. "So, this was supposed to be a very private service. Do you know anyone else who's coming?" I ask. What I really want to ask is how the hell she was invited, but again there's a time and a place for everything.

"My agent is very good friends with Phoebe's agent. I know how small the guest list is. I had a full schedule today, but nothing is as important as this." She looks around and waves at a woman three rows behind us. "Excuse me," she says. "I need to say hello to another dear friend."

I watch as she falls into the arms of the woman, just like she did mine. I sit back down next to Raven who has once again closed her eyes. A few seconds later, the organ begins to play, and the other guests find their seats. James sits down across the aisle from us, next to the tuxedo guy.

The pastor begins to speak and delivers a few prayers along with the eulogy. I listen to his calming words and tribute to my friend, but I quickly realize that I know everything he's saying. It almost sounds like he's reading from Wikipedia, sharing details about Phoebe that most of the public already knows. At the same time, I'm sitting next to a woman who was Phoebe's own flesh and blood but didn't have a relationship with her.

I truly feel like I knew her better than anyone. I'm the one she told about the beach trips she took with her mother during her childhood, and how they would get a souvenir T-shirt from every place they visited. She also told me stories about getting dressed up to watch the Emmys, Tonys, and Oscars when she was a little girl, and how she was determined from a very young age to become an actress. These are the private moments of her life that she chose to share with me.

∾

In the end, after describing the well-known details of Phoebe's professional life, the pastor delivers a beautiful service, and I know Phoebe would be pleased. As soon as the service ends, people begin to exit. I'm about to leave when James and the tuxedo guy approach me.

"Casey, this is Judd Dawson. He's been Phoebe's attorney for many years."

Judd reaches out to shake my hand. "Hello, Ms. Cooper. I was going to reach out to you, but James told me you were here, so it saves me a phone call."

What? Why would he want to talk to me? "Um, okay."

"There will be a reading of Phoebe's will, and your name is on the list to be in attendance."

I try to process what he's saying. "I'm sorry. Why do I have to attend? I wasn't—"

"Phoebe had specific instructions," he interrupts. "There were four people she included, and you're one of them. We will do the reading next Monday. My assistant will reach out to you once I finalize the time."

I glance at James who appears to be distracted or—irritated? I'm actually a bit flummoxed by his expression.

"I'll see you on Monday," Judd says before walking away.

James also walks away without another word.

I sit back down on the bench by myself and try to collect my thoughts. Never in a million years would I expect to be included in Phoebe's will. She was my friend, the sister I never had, but I never wanted anything more from her than her friendship. I bury my face in my hands.

I sit quietly for a few minutes as I try to process this new information. I finally lift my head and glance at the white casket in front of me. I get up and walk toward it, resting my hand on the top.

"Rest in peace, my friend," I whisper. I dab the corners of my eyes and turn around to pick up my bag.

When I look up, I notice James and Raven standing close to one another, talking in the back corner of the church. James is shaking his head, and it's very obvious that he's not happy about something. Raven also looks upset, and then I see her brush his shoulder with her fingertips.

Something about their interaction rubs me wrong. Why is she touching him like that? When James initially told me about Raven, he made it seem like he had never spoken to her before Phoebe's death. And he acted so defensive of her when I suggested she had an ulterior motive for showing up here. He obviously knew how to get in contact with her because he told her about Phoebe's death. Their conversation screams there is more going on there than two people who have only just met.

James seemed unhappy to hear that I was in the will. Could he be sharing that with Raven now? I have my suspicions that James knows more about Phoebe's death, but what if Raven is somehow connected as well?

I pause and look back at Phoebe's casket. Once again, I get the strong feeling that what I saw in the Ambassador Suite was a setup. And now, after seeing James and Raven with their heads together, I'm more convinced than ever that he's not being completely forthcoming with what he knows.

"Don't worry, Phoebe. I will find out the truth, I promise," I say under my breath.

Chapter Twelve

*T*he next day, I'm back at the hotel waiting for Detective Cain to meet me. I reached out to him after witnessing the interaction between James and Raven at Phoebe's funeral. I also let Max know I contacted him because I don't want it to seem like I'm trying to hide anything. I hate not knowing what's going on, but like Kendall reminded me last night, the police don't have to tell me anything.

I take a sip of my coffee, which is the last thing I should be drinking right now. I'm so amped up on caffeine that I'm sure I'm tearing up my insides as we speak. Not to mention, I haven't been able to eat, so my whole nervous system is in a state of sheer misery.

I woke up several times during the night, thinking about Phoebe's will and James' reaction. At first, I was confused by his reaction, but judging by the way he left without acknowledging me, I think it's safe to say that he was as surprised as I was that I was included. I also tried searching online to see if there was anything that would tie James and

Raven together, but I couldn't find anything. The only thing I found on Raven's social media profile was a post about spending time with an amazing man and his family. But that was several months ago.

I am just starting to scroll through my phone when Detective Cain and Max enter the conference room together. "Thanks for meeting with me," I say shaking his hand. "Hi, Max."

"Casey," he says with a nod.

"Your call came in at the perfect time. I have some new information about the case to share with you."

The butterflies in my stomach begin stretching their wings.

"Just a reminder, please keep these new developments to yourself."

I nod my head in agreement.

"The results came back from the toxicology reports. The reports showed she had extremely deadly levels of narcotics in her system."

My heart sinks.

"There's no way she took all those drugs," I insist. "I don't believe—"

Detective Cain holds up his hand. "But, considering the missing package and the specific position of her body, we still have reason to believe there was another party or parties involved, and it was a set up to look like a suicide."

A feeling of relief washes over me. "Good, because I think

there's more going on here. The reason I called you is because I witnessed a very strange conversation going on with James and Phoebe's cousin, Raven, at her funeral. They weren't acting like two people who had just met. But when James told me he contacted her, he made it sound as if they didn't know each other. And because Phoebe never told me she had a cousin, I questioned him about her. He acted really defensive. I really think he knows more about her death than he's admitting."

Detective Cain clears his throat. "Regardless of the conversation you saw between them, Ms. Phord's assistant was not in the hotel that afternoon, and we've confirmed his alibi."

"Was his alibi that he was with her cousin?" I ask half joking.

He shakes his head. "He was out of town visiting family about two hours away. This has been confirmed after speaking with a family member."

"Well he may not have been physically here in the hotel, but he could still be involved," I say, raising my voice. "Isn't it possible that a family member could lie for him?"

I glance at Max, who's now staring at me.

"Well, yes," Detective Cain says.

"I apologize if I'm being rude, but something doesn't feel right about any of this."

Detective Cain smiles. "I don't think you're being rude. I understand why you're upset. I also want to let you know that we've confirmed the package was delivered to the hotel that day, and we've been in contact with the shipping service. Now we're waiting to get more information on its contents and where it originated."

"Does that mean I'm no longer a person of interest?" I ask, with an edge in my voice.

"Casey—" Max says softly.

Detective Cain nods. "That's correct. The autopsy report also showed Ms. Phord had already been dead for approximately two hours when you entered her room around six thirty p.m."

Okay, so that means the person who killed her was in her room around the same time I was dealing with Mikenzie/Ruby and her many requests. Her package had already been delivered. Ugh. I should've taken it to her sooner. But this still begs the question, who was in her room earlier in the day? This causes the hair to stand up on the back of my neck.

I mentally go through our guest list. The only person I know of with any kind of personal connection to Phoebe is Mikenzie, but I was on the phone with her off and on for most of the day. I chew on my bottom lip. What if it was someone who worked here at the hotel? But who would have a reason to kill her and stage her body?

"Ms. Cooper, we know how close you are to this situation, but you need to use discretion. Considering how high profile this case is, we don't want this information leaked to the press. That's why we've not gone public with the new findings."

Well, at least they're trying to be discreet. Unfortunately, by doing so, Phoebe's name is being dragged through the mud.

"I know this is frustrating for you," he adds. "It's a very

unfortunate situation, but please be patient. I assure you, we're doing everything we can to get answers. We've been going through her phone, laptop, anything that could lead us to some an—"

The sound of Detective Cain's phone interrupts our conversation. He excuses himself, leaving me sitting quietly with Max.

"I don't care what they say," I tell him. "Someone who was in this hotel that day killed her."

"Casey, I think you're way too close to this situation," Max whispers. "You need—"

"I don't need time off," I reply before he even gets the words out. "I need to help my friend."

"I'm sorry to cut this short, but I have to follow up on a few things," Detective Cain says.

"Thank you for keeping us updated," Max says.

"Yes, thank you," I add.

He gives me a nod. "We will continue to search for the answers you're looking for. Just be patient, and I promise we will uncover the truth."

As soon as he's gone, I exhale loudly.

"You okay?" Max asks.

I don't say anything for a few seconds. "I think so. It's definitely a relief knowing that my name is cleared from any involvement."

"I can imagine," he says. "I still think you need to take some time off."

"I just had a day off yesterday."

"One day, and you attended Phoebe's funeral. I wouldn't exactly consider that a break."

"I wasn't here, so it counts as a break from work," I say, squaring off my shoulders and folding my arms.

We quietly stare at each other until he cracks a smile. "Are you always this stubborn?" he asks.

My shoulders relax slightly. "It depends." I pause. "I haven't been in this position very long, and you just started here. There's a lot of work to be done, and to be quite honest, sitting at home alone isn't going to make me forget what happened."

He gives me a thoughtful look. "I understand. I just want to assure you that your job won't be in jeopardy if you take a few days to clear your head."

I smile. "That's good to know. Truthfully, as pathetic as it sounds, this job is basically my life."

"I can relate. I gave up any kind of a personal life when I began managing hotels. Throw in the long hours and extensive travel, it makes it near impossible to do anything else."

I take a deep breath. "The Fountain Rose has been in such upheaval since the scandal with Colton happened. I have so many ideas and suggestions, I don't know where to begin."

"Okay, so let's do it." He stops. "I mean, let's discuss them.

Make a list of your ideas, and we'll talk about them as soon as you're ready."

"That would be awesome," I say, grabbing his arm. I can't help but notice how muscular his bicep is under my hand, and before I realize what I'm doing, I squeeze his arm. I seriously want to die. I quickly pull my hand away. *Damn coffee.* "I'm sorry," I exclaim. "I didn't mean to—that was really embarrassing."

He laughs. "Don't be embarrassed. I'm either working or working out. Sometimes I sleep."

"I can tell you work out a lot." Okay, I'm done. "Um, I better get back to work before Belinda reports me to my boss."

He laughs. "Let her report you."

"I will compile that list for you. I have notes everywhere right now, in my phone, on sticky notes, in my computer. Thanks for being here with the detective. It's really helpful."

Before I embarrass myself any further, or touch him in any other way, I escape the conference room and return to the safety of my little office. Maybe I should take him up on his offer and take some time off. One thing is for sure though, I'm very drawn to him, and I don't know how to stop it.

I wish Phoebe were here. She would know what to do.

Chapter Thirteen

"*W*hy are you hiding in here?" Peyton asks, poking her head into my office.

I groan. "Because I'm in no condition to communicate with other humans today."

She raises her eyebrows and opens the door all the way. As soon as she walks in, I notice her top button is open, and her scarf is untied and hanging loosely around her neck.

"Are you on the clock yet?" I ask.

She laughs wickedly. "Not yet. I just felt like getting a rise out of Belinda today." She begins to tie her scarf around her neck.

Those two really do go out of their way to purposely antagonize each other. One of these days, it's going to reach a boiling point. I mentally add the situation to my list of things to discuss with Max, again. I know he told me to figure out a creative way for Belinda and Peyton to work together, but I'm beginning to think it's just a bad idea.

"You and Belinda need to chill. Enough is enough," I tell her.

"Come on, Casey. It's not like our dislike for each other is anything new."

I rub my temples.

She gives me a curious look. "Casey, don't take this wrong."

Ahhh … it's never good when someone utters those words.

"Have you considered talking to someone? There's nothing wrong with seeing a shrink. I mean, you found a dead body. That's major trauma."

"I'm okay."

She cocks her head to the side. "Are you sure? I'm worried you're working too hard. Maybe you should take some time to deal with everything that's going on? You never even told me about the funeral."

I don't know how to respond to her questions. Should I be curled up in my bed in the fetal position? How am I'm supposed to feel or act? The last I checked, there weren't rules about how to deal with grief.

"I appreciate your concern. The funeral was nice, very small. I'm dealing with it—every day it feels different."

I don't tell her that I was asked to be at the reading of Phoebe's will. Some things are better kept to myself.

"I do still think there's something up with James," I tell her.

"It wouldn't surprise me." She runs her fingers through her hair. "I bet the police are missing something."

I think about what Detective Cain said about confirming James' alibi. "What makes you say that?"

She shrugs. "Because they always miss something in those detective shows."

I giggle. "I guess that's true, but that's TV. This is real life."

She looks at her phone and jumps up from her chair. "Oh crap, I've got to clock in. We can talk more later, and I still want to hear more about the funeral."

"Thanks for checking on me," I call.

"Welcome," she calls back.

The police are missing something, and I'm sure it has to do with James and Raven.

When I step off the elevator onto the twenty-seventh floor, my heart starts to race. I haven't been up here since the night I found Phoebe's body. It's been cleaned multiple times, and James packed up her things. It's eerily quiet now, but I still need to see the room to get some closure.

I swipe my master key and enter the Ambassador Suite. I look around, and of course there isn't a single pillow out of place. I make my way into the bedroom and pause at the door. Suddenly the memory of seeing Phoebe's designer gown-clad body flashes through my mind. I shake my head to make the image go away.

After gathering my composure, I begin opening drawers and

looking under the furniture. As expected, there isn't a trace of Phoebe left here.

I sit down on the edge of the bed, and a feeling of regret takes over. I should have come up here sooner, at least before the police cleaned the room out.

"Hello?" a voice calls.

I jump up from the bed and walk into the living room, where I find Alfie standing by the door. "Casey? Are you okay?"

"Hey, Alfie. Yeah, I just—" I pause while I think of how to explain. "I haven't been up here since ... and I guess I wanted to see it again." I shift from one foot to the other. "What are you doing here?"

"I saw you get off the elevator. I wanted to make sure everything was all right."

"I'm fine. Sorry to alarm you."

He shakes his head. "Don't worry about it. Peyton mentioned you were having a hard day."

Of course she did.

"I'm just drained," I tell him. "Max keeps telling me to take a few days off, but honestly, I prefer to stay busy."

"You really should," he says. "And if you have the okay from the new boss, why not take advantage of it?"

"You're probably right."

"I am right."

I look around the suite, and a feeling of sadness comes over me. If only I knew what was happening in those last few hours of Phoebe's life.

"Are you still searching for answers about Phoebe's death? Is that why you're in here?"

"Yes. I was hoping to come up here and find something that might help me make some sense of all of this."

"What did you think you're going to find that the police haven't found? They've been through every inch of this room."

I shrug. "You never know."

He gives me a questioning look. "Casey, don't get upset at me for saying this, but I think you're wasting your time. And being in here is only making you relive what happened."

Why is he so quick to dismiss any other possibilities? I don't understand why he would try to convince me to give up searching. Does he know more than he's saying? I take another glance around the room, hoping something else will jump out at me, but nothing does.

"Did the police ever find out what happened to the security footage from that day?"

He shakes his head. "No, unfortunately not. As of right now, there's no proof of anyone else being in her room that day," he says. "I'm sorry, Casey."

"How is that possible? " I wail.

He hangs his head. "I don't know. I wish I had some answers."

I chew on my lip. He's supposed to be in charge of the security at our hotel. How could someone get in and out of this suite without a trace?

"Casey, I really think you're taking on too much right now. Let me walk you back to your office," he says.

It's clear he's trying to change the subject, but I agree, and we make our way to the elevator.

"I don't need to take a vacation," I exclaim as the elevator descends. "I appreciate that you're all concerned, but it feels like people are trying to get rid of me."

He looks surprised. "That's not what I'm trying to do. I just think you're wasting a lot of energy on something that's out of your control. It's the authorities' job to find out what happened, not yours."

We step out of the elevator and into the lobby.

"Phoebe was my friend, and I'm going to help get justice for her no matter what it takes," I insist.

"Excuse me, Casey," Belinda interrupts. She has her arms folded tightly against her chest. "Mikenzie or Ruby Carson has requested that you call her. She says she's left multiple messages, and you haven't responded." She gives me a familiar disapproving look.

"Thanks. I'll reach out to her right away," I tell her. "I'll see you later, Alfie."

As I make my way to my office, I replay my conversation with Alfie. I understand he's on edge because of what's been going on, but something is off with him. The more I think about it, the more I'm questioning the "lack" of security footage. Did something get erased on purpose? Could the cameras have been tampered with?

I listen to Mikenzie's message. "Hello, Casey. I'm sorry I wasn't able to talk with you at the funeral. It was just too difficult." I roll my eyes. "Anyway, please tell your staff that I would like my turndown service an hour later from now on."

That's the end of her message. That was her urgent need to talk to me? I hang up the phone and sigh loudly.

I still don't understand how she was able to attend Phoebe's funeral or why she wanted to. Maybe she just wanted to be "seen" or make it look like she and Phoebe had a friendship. I think back to the last conversation we all had with Phoebe, and this reminds me that Mikenzie and her friend knew how important that package was to Phoebe. Could one of them have slipped in and taken it just out of curiosity? Is there a chance the package disappearing isn't connected to Phoebe's murder after all? And what's up with Alfie? Ugh. There are way too many questions that need answers, and I'm determined to get them.

I dial Mikenzie's room, but there's no answer, so I leave a message.

"Hi, Mikenzie, or Ruby, it's Casey. Please call extension 112 when you have a moment. I'm getting ready to leave for the night, but I will be here in the morning. Thanks."

There's no way I'm taking time off now. I'm staying right here in The Fountain Rose, and I'm keeping my promise to Phoebe. I'm going to find out who did this to her.

Chapter Fourteen

"*C*asey?"

I'm walking down a dark street when I hear my name being called.

"Casey," the voice repeats with a sense of urgency.

"Who's there?"

"Please help me," the voice pleads.

"I'm coming," I yell into the darkness.

I'm trying to run, but my legs won't move. I feel like I'm stuck in the same spot, my body moving in slow motion.

"Please help me."

"I'm trying!" I shout.

I scream and suddenly find myself in my living room. I sit up, my heart racing, and kick off the blanket. An episode of *Friends* is on the TV, and I check the time on the screen. It's only eleven thirty, but it feels like it's the middle of the night. I vaguely remember coming home from work a few hours ago and sitting down on the couch.

I hear my phone buzzing from the kitchen, so I peel myself off the couch to get it.

When I pick up my phone, I have three texts from Peyton waiting for me.

OMG! I HAVE TO TELL YOU SOMETHING.

CALL ME. IT'S URGENT.

WHERE ARE YOU? HURRY!

My pulse begins to race. What's so important?

I try calling her back, but it goes straight to her voicemail, so I leave a message.

"Peyton, it's me. I fell asleep. What's going on? Call me back."

I also send her a text.

JUST TRIED CALLING YOU. WHAT'S HAPPENING?

I walk back into the living room, staring at my phone. I jump about ten feet in the air when I notice Kendall standing there.

"What the hell? When did you get here?" I yell.

"About an hour ago. You were asleep, and I didn't want to wake you, so I covered you with the blanket."

I dramatically fall down on the couch. My heart was already

racing from the dream, but now it feels like it's about to burst out of my chest.

"Sorry I scared you," she says, sitting on the loveseat and curling her legs under her. "Are you okay? You look a little pale."

I glance at my phone. "Yeah, I just had a weird dream, and then I got some texts from Peyton at the hotel. She says she has to tell me something important."

She raises her eyebrows. "Isn't that the girl who always has drama?"

I nod. "Yes. She's gotten much better though. Ever since she and Alfie have been *flirting*."

I guess that's what they're still doing. With everything going on, I haven't asked for an update. I look at my phone. Still no response so I put it back down next to me and lean my head back against the couch.

"That dream really freaked me out."

"What was it about?"

I tell her about the dream and describe the voice begging me for help. "It's probably nothing," I say. "Maybe my mind is playing tricks on me because of everything that's been happening. Max wants me to take a few days off, and I'm starting to think I should."

"Who's Max?"

"Our new GM at the hotel," I tell her. I don't give her any more details about him or his physical attributes. It's better if I put those out of my mind completely.

"I think a few days off would really help you," she says.

"That's what everyone keeps saying. Although I'm starting to think they're just trying to get rid of me."

She smiles. "Paranoia is a terrible thing, isn't it? I was so paranoid after what happened at Blossom."

"So you think they're just being nice?"

"Probably."

I groan.

"I know what you're thinking," she says. "You're thinking that if you take time off, you're not being helpful. And you want to fix everything that's going wrong."

She's right.

"Casey, you can't. As much as you want to be the one to help and solve this, sometimes you have to take a few steps back."

"I understand what you're saying, but I owe it to Phoebe to do everything I can," I reply.

"You can still help her, but one day isn't going to change anything."

"Ah, it sounds so logical coming from you."

I grab my phone and send Max a text letting him know that I'm taking tomorrow off. Maybe this is exactly what I need. The hotel will be just fine without me for one day.

"Casey?"

I open my eyes to see Kendall standing next to my bed.

"Hey," I mumble.

"I'm sorry to wake you."

"It's okay," I tell her, closing my eyes. *Why is she waking me up? She knows I'm taking the day off.*

"Ryan just called and told me something happened at the hotel."

A few seconds later I sit up. "What?" I rub my eyes vigorously so I can focus. Kendall sits down on the edge of the bed.

"I'm sorry, Casey."

"Sorry about what? What happened?"

She tightens her lips. "Apparently, there was an accident. Peyton fell down a flight of stairs and—"

"And what?"

"Ryan said she landed on the marble floor." She pauses and clears her throat. "She's dead, Casey."

"No!" I shout then cover my mouth with my hands. This can't be happening. I jump out of my bed and look for my phone as the tears begin to fall from my eyes. I find it on the floor. I have one text from Max telling me he was glad I was not coming in, but that was from last night. Peyton never called me back or responded to my texts. My heart is beating fast against the walls of my chest. She said she had to tell me something important. Now she's dead? What are the chances this wasn't an accident?

I begin to shake and sob uncontrollably as I sit down on the edge of the bed.

Kendall puts her arms around me and gently rubs my back. "I'm so sorry, Casey."

"I don't think it was an accident," I wail between my tears. "Look at her texts. She was begging me to call her."

Kendall scrolls through my phone.

"I'll call Ryan right away."

"I need to get to the hotel," I say, standing up.

"No, you don't," she insists. "Let's talk to Ryan first and see what he says."

"Okay," I reluctantly agree through my tears.

I follow Kendall to the living room and listen from the couch while she tells Ryan about the texts Peyton sent me. Maybe Peyton found something out about what happened to Phoebe. Is that what was so important? Did she find out who killed her? Or even worse, what if Peyton knew something about Phoebe's death all along? Peyton knew about the package, and she was so curious to know what the contents were. Was that what her texts were about? What if she was trying to tell me the truth and someone wanted to stop her?

My mind goes through this scenario again, and the more I think about, my gut tells me that's not why she was texting me. She wouldn't have kept that secret.

"Ryan's on his way over," Kendall says, bringing me a cup of coffee.

I take a sip and nod. "Thanks."

She sits down next to me on the couch.

"I have a feeling this is connected to Phoebe somehow," I tell her.

Kendall chews on her lower lip.

I sigh and dab the corner of my eyes. "There's something up with her assistant, James. And this long-lost cousin that she never mentioned. I saw them with their heads together after the funeral."

She nods slowly. "That would make sense. He's had access to everything in her private life. Her schedule, and of course her money."

I rub my forehead. "Well, he definitely wasn't happy when he found out I was included in the reading of her will."

Kendall's mouth falls open. "You're in her will?"

I shrug my shoulders. "I guess. Her attorney approached me after the funeral. James seemed very surprised."

She shakes her head. "It sounds like he's a very viable suspect."

"I think so, but apparently he has an alibi."

"Okay, so maybe someone in the hotel could be working with him."

"That's what I think."

Kendall puts her hand to her mouth and stares off into space. "Casey, doesn't your fancy hotel have security cameras? There isn't any video of someone going into Phoebe's room?"

"Of course. There are cameras in all the halls, but there wasn't any footage from that day. Supposedly the whole system is pretty dated, and they think it malfunctioned."

"That's really strange."

"I think so too. I'm thinking it was erased or maybe the cameras were tampered with? It's just too convenient that there's nothing. The strangest thing is that when I went to the suite to look around yesterday, Alfie, our head of security, showed up."

She raises her eyebrows. "And what did he say?"

"He told me I was wasting my time because the police had already been there. Then he told me he thought I needed to take some time off."

I loudly blow my nose into one of the tissues she brought me. "Peyton and Alfie have been seeing each other!" I exclaim. "What if she found out something, and that's why she was texting me?"

Did Peyton discover that Alfie had tampered with the cameras? Or even worse, did she discover that he killed Phoebe? Could Alfie have been working with James this whole time?

I drop my face into my hands. "I don't know, Kendall. What reason could Alfie have to want to kill Phoebe?"

"Money," she suggests.

I nod as I replay the last few weeks, and the day James came to me suddenly pops into my mind. "Phoebe's assistant came to the hotel after she died. Alfie was very adamant that he be present for our conversation. Maybe he was nervous that James would tell me something that would incriminate him."

I continue to think of everything. "There's also the missing package that I took to Phoebe's room that day. The police never found it, and Alfie did come into the suite after me. He said he never noticed it ..."

A knock on the door interrupts our conversation. Kendall hurries to the door. "Ryan?"

"It's me."

She opens the door and wraps her arms around his neck before joining me in the living room.

"Hey, Casey, how you are holding up?" he asks, sitting down on the couch next to me.

"Barely," I say, my voice shaking. "Peyton sent me a few urgent texts last night, and I missed them. I tried calling her back, but —she never answered."

Tears begin to fall again while Kendall rubs my back.

"I think she was pushed down those stairs," I blurt out in between sobs. "Look at my texts. She said she needed to talk to me. Maybe she found out something about Phoebe's murder."

Kendall hands him my phone, and he begins scrolling through the text messages. "She asks you to call her, but she doesn't say what it's about. We don't know for sure that she wanted to talk to you about Phoebe."

I wipe under my eyes with my fingers. "No, she doesn't, but don't you think it could be a possibility?" I ask. "I was just telling Kendall that I'm wondering if Alfie is involved in all of this. I'm thinking he could be helping someone because he has access to every corner of that hotel. He was one of the first people to arrive in Phoebe's suite after I found her. It feels like he's trying to get me to stop searching for answers. And what about there being no footage from that day? He's in charge of our security." I pause and let out a deep sigh. "Detective Cain told me that James' alibi checks out, but isn't it still possible he was working with someone at the hotel?"

He nods thoughtfully.

"And Alfie and Peyton were romantically involved," I tell him. "Maybe she found out something about him, and that's what she was trying to tell me."

Kendall has been quietly listening to our conversation. The three of us don't say anything while Ryan continues to make notes in his notebook. The only sound is coming from my sniffling.

"Okay, I'll get with Detective Cain," Ryan says, closing his notebook. "He's at the hotel now investigating Peyton's death."

Poor Peyton. I wonder if she came across some information by accident. Maybe she was in the wrong place at the wrong time—like the top of the stairs?

Once again, I'm too late to help my friend. My mind wanders to what was happening right before Peyton *fell*. Was she confronting someone? Was that when she was frantically trying to get in touch with me?

"I need to get to the hotel," I announce, jumping up from the couch. "I need to find out what happened to Peyton. Another tragic event has occurred, and it's my job to take care of our guests."

"Casey," Kendall says, trying to stop me. "I don't think you're in any state to …"

I hold up my hand. "I'm going."

Chapter Fifteen

I leave two messages for Max letting him know I'm on my way to the hotel. I try my best to look as presentable as possible. Unfortunately, the tears that continue to escape my eyes don't make my makeup application easy.

Honestly, I feel like I'm stuck in a nightmare that I can't wake up from. That dream I had feels even more real now, like it was a premonition or a vision. I'm beginning to wonder if Peyton was trying to send me a message, or maybe Phoebe was pleading with me not to give up on finding out the truth.

Well, I'm *not* giving up. I'm going to do everything in my power to find out what really happened to my friends. The reading of Phoebe's will is in two days, and I'm praying that I get some answers there. Or at least something that will lead me in the right direction.

When I arrive at The Fountain Rose, I push my way through the photographers and into the hotel lobby. Max, Belinda, and

Sami from our reservations team are at the front desk fielding questions from guests.

According to Detective Ryan, a guest found Peyton at the bottom of the east tower staircase early this morning. The east tower is off the beaten path and farther away from the guest amenities. It doesn't get as much traffic because most guests use the elevator that goes directly to the lobby, which is much more convenient.

Max frowns when he sees me approach the counter. I'm sure I'm going to receive a lecture about being here, but I don't care. Who would have thought my boss would demand I stay home instead of coming to work? Max finishes with a guest and motions for me to follow him. I follow his lead, and we quietly walk to his office.

"Why are you here?" he asks as soon as he closes the door behind me. "You were supposed to be taking today off."

I stand up straight and jut out my chin. "You need me here, and I—" My lips start to tremble at the thought of Peyton. Crap, the tears are already coming, and there's no chance I'm stopping them.

Before I know it, Max wraps his arms around me, and I let the tears fall onto his crisp white shirt. "I'm so sorry about Peyton. Such a terrible accident," he says softly.

I pull away from his chest, forcing his massive arms to loosen around me. Thankfully, he doesn't let me go completely.

"What if it wasn't an accident?" I ask. "What if she was pushed down those stairs?"

Max gives me a sympathetic look. "Casey, she was wearing

three-inch high-heeled shoes. The police think she either tripped or her heel got caught."

"Or maybe someone pushed her," I repeat.

He finally releases his arms from around me. "That sure is a heavy accusation. What makes you think someone pushed her?"

He looks confused, so I show him the texts Peyton sent me the night before. "I'm wondering if she found out something about what happened to Phoebe, and that's why she wanted to talk to me so badly."

He shrugs. "You can't be sure her texts were about Phoebe."

Ryan said the same thing. It's so frustrating that no one else can see what's happening here. "And you can't be sure they aren't," I scoff.

He raises his eyebrows but doesn't reply.

"Have the police said anything about security footage from last night?" I ask, thinking about them not finding any the day Phoebe died.

I can almost see the wheels turning in Max's brain. "They haven't said yet." He sits on the edge of his desk.

"Come on, Max. How can there be no footage from the day Phoebe died? That's certainly convenient, don't you think?"

I can't be the only person who's considered this to be a possibility. Although I'm sure the police have … at least I hope they have. Alfie told me they questioned him after Phoebe's death. Again, I know they haven't told us everything, and why would they?

Max picks up his phone and scrolls through it. He begins typing. "Okay, I'm sending the detective a text. He was here this morning, so let's get his thoughts before we start blowing up Alfie."

I fold my arms. "I'm not waiting for Detective Cain. I'm going to talk to Alfie now."

I turn and head for the door when I feel his hand around my arm. "Whoa. Just hold on until—"

"No," I insist. "Enough time has passed. The person who did this is going to get away with murder, maybe not just once but twice," I say, throwing my hands in the air. "I can't sit by while the media continues to say horrible things about Phoebe, and this hotel doesn't need any more negative publicity."

Max puts his hand on my shoulders and leans down to look me in the eyes.

I feel a pulse shoot through my body. I guess it's true that traumatic situations can do strange things to you. Although, I can't deny my attraction to Max.

"I understand how you're feeling. Two people you cared about are dead."

"Yes, they are …" My lips begin to quiver again, so I close my eyes and push back my tears.

"I'm just trying to tell you to take things slow. Barging into Alfie's office and screaming accusations isn't going to get you the answers you want."

I know he's right.

"And if there's any truth in what you're suggesting, you also need to be careful, so I'm coming with you."

I hold up one hand. "No. I think I should go alone. I won't just barge in and accuse him, but I want to talk to him. And I'm not sure if you know this, but he and Peyton were romantically involved. They were trying to keep it quiet because of everything that went down with the last staff members who …" I stop talking as I look into Max's eyes which are now locked with mine. "Anyway, I'll just tell him that I wanted to check on him. I'll be okay."

Before he can try to talk me out of it, I leave and make a beeline for the security offices, Max closely following behind.

When I arrive at Alfie's office, my heart starts to beat faster against the wall of my chest.

I knock softly and wait. There's no answer, so I knock louder … still no answer. When I try to open the door, it's locked. Crap.

I look at Max "casually" walking down the hall. "Can you unlock this for me?"

He sighs as he continues to walk toward me. He unlocks the door, and I give him a grateful smile.

When I walk into the office, I'm met with lots of buttons, computers, and TV monitors. I've been here a few times in the past, but of course I don't have a clue how anything works. I stand back as I watch the monitors switch to different areas in the hotel. I can't help but notice how messy it is in here. There are stacks of files and papers everywhere. A collection of togo containers and cups are all over the place. It's actually pretty gross.

I wonder what Max would say about this. His office is completely spotless. I tiptoe toward the desk and with two fingers flip through some papers. I don't see anything other than boring reports, graphs, and notes. I'm shifting everything back to how I found it when something catches my eye. All I can see is the corner of a picture that's sticking out from under the desk calendar. I pull it out so I can see the entire thing. It looks like it's been ripped out of an old magazine. The title reads, "Up and Coming Actress Phoebe Phord Lands Leading Role on New Daytime Serial, *Love and Eternity.*"

Wow, why does Alfie have this? I'm pretty sure this thing is older than he is.

I hear keys jingling outside the door, so I quickly shove the article into my pocket and sit down in the desk chair. I make myself busy with my phone.

The door opens, and Alfie stops dead in his tracks. "Casey, what are you doing in here?" The smell of french fries begins to permeate the room as soon as he walks in.

"I was waiting for you," I tell him. "Max let me in. I wanted to check on you after ..."

It could be my imagination, but it looks like he quickly scans the room. Maybe he's checking to see if I moved anything. Although I don't know how he would notice unless his mess was in some kind of order. It's a good thing I tried to leave everything as it was, just in case.

"Yeah, I was going to call you about Peyton, but Max told me you finally decided to take time off, and I didn't want to upset you further." He puts his fast food bags down and sits in the chair next to me.

"I was planning on it until I heard about Peyton. What about you? I mean, how are you?"

He clasps his hands together and lowers his head. "I—I think I'm in shock. Did you hear what happened? The police think she fell from the top of the staircase. And with the impact—" He clears his throat.

I close my eyes and hold up my hand to stop him as tears fill my eyes. "I just don't understand why this is happening."

He presses his lips together and looks away.

"Did the cameras catch anything?" I ask. "I mean, did they show how it happened?" I'm trying to think of the best way to ask these questions without shooting accusations at him like Max said.

He clears his throat. "Yes, well, we have the footage of her at the bottom of the stairs. Her neck—"

I hold up my hand. The image that pops into my head makes me nauseous. "So, there's no video with her actually falling down the stairs?"

He narrows his eyebrows. "No, not the fall, but there's video of her on the ground at the bottom of the stairs. Remember, the cameras are constantly on rotation switching to different angles and areas."

I furrow my brow while I try to process everything. It's all so overwhelming. "What are the chances? I mean first Phoebe dies here in our hotel, and now Peyton. It's just too much," I exclaim as I rub my temples vigorously.

He sits up straight as he shifts around in his chair. "Casey? What would Peyton falling down the stairs have to do with Phoebe's death?"

"I don't know exactly. But two of my friends are dead, and I'm trying to process it. In the meantime, I have a hotel full of guests that I need to pay attention to, but I'm barely holding it together myself. We've had two people turn up dead in a matter of weeks, and I want to know what happened to them."

Alfie lets out a frustrated sigh. "We all do."

"I still think—"

"Casey, stop! You need to stay out of this and let them do their job," he interrupts, raising his voice.

I watch as his chest rises, and his cheeks turn red. "Alfie."

He shakes his head. "I'm sorry. I shouldn't have yelled, I'm just under a lot of pressure, and now Peyton is gone."

What kind of pressure? Is he feeling pressure because he really doesn't know what's happened? Or are the walls closing in on him?

"I know." I rub my forehead. I'm starting to get a massive headache from crying so much. "Peyton tried messaging me last night, and I missed her texts. I feel so terrible that I wasn't able to talk to her one last time. Maybe if I had, things would be different? Just like Phoebe ... maybe if I had gone to her room sooner she'd still be alive."

I watch him to gauge his reaction. He loudly clears his throat and looks away. "Don't think that way. Her accident is not your fault," he says softly, putting his hand on my arm. "If anything, I should've done a better job of protecting everyone."

I try not to wince at the thought that I'm alone with a person who could be connected to these two deaths. I think about the article about Phoebe I just found on his desk. I quickly stand up. "You're right. Peyton's fall is not my fault. That's why I'm going to do whatever I can to help the police find answers."

I use my terrible headache as an excuse to leave in a hurry, and I race back to my office with my hand in my pocket.

Chapter Sixteen

"Casey?"

I stop in my tracks and turn around to see Belinda staring at me.

"Why are you running?" she asks, eyeing me curiously.

"I just remembered I had to follow up on something." I walk toward Belinda. Even *she* looks out of sorts today.

"You don't look so good, Casey."

My face falls. "It's been a rough day."

Her expression twists from sadness to irritation. "You know that Peyton and I never got along. I wish—" She nervously fixes her scarf. "I wish things could have been different, but it's too late now."

I pat her on the shoulder. "Don't feel bad. Sometimes people don't mesh well."

She nods and looks away. "Anyway, I can't change the past.

For now, I need to focus on what I'm here to do." She heads toward the lobby, allowing me to finally escape to my office.

When I'm safely inside, I pull the magazine clipping out of my pocket and read through it. It talks about Phoebe landing the leading role by beating out another actress who was up for it. Phoebe had worked with the producers on a previous project. It doesn't give more information than that. I sit back in my chair and think about why Alfie has this, and why it was hidden under the calendar. Did he find it somewhere in the hotel? Or did someone give it to him? James maybe? I wonder if Peyton saw this in his office.

I read through it again two more times to see if something stands out. I think about Phoebe and the Emmys she won for that same role. I'm thinking there has to be a connection.

I grab my phone to call Detective Cain. He doesn't answer, so I leave a message.

I rub my forehead with my hands. My head is now absolutely pounding. I locate a bottle of headache relief tablets in my drawer and take a few before I fold up the article and slip it back into my pocket. I should hide it somewhere but decide to keep it with me.

Sighing, I lay my head down on my desk while I wait for some relief from my headache. It's so quiet in here. I think about all the times Peyton has barged into my office. This causes me to tear up once more, knowing that will never happen again.

I wait a few minutes and then listen to my messages. I make a few notes until I hear Mikenzie's voice.

"Casey, we have to talk. They told me at the front desk that you were out of the office for a while. When will you be back? Call me."

I groan. I know I need to call her back, and I will, just not right this second. I sit back in my chair and turn from side to side while listening to the silence. It's almost deafening.

When I was offered this new career path, I knew things were going to be different around here, just not *this* different. I still feel like I'm trapped in that nightmare from last night, and I just wish I could wake up. Unfortunately, I'm not dreaming. This madness is happening all around me, and I have to figure out how to stop it.

I'm about to return Mikenzie's message when I hear a knock on my office door. I place my hand on my pocket to make sure the magazine article is still there. Wow, Kendall was definitely right about paranoia taking over.

"Come in."

Belinda opens the door. "Do you have a second?"

She walks in before I respond.

"Sami is watching the front desk," she says, sitting down in the chair across from me. "Casey, I've been thinking … I've been really insensitive to you lately. I know how close you were with Phoebe, and now with Peyton's accident, I shouldn't have been so difficult."

I shake my head. "Belinda, it's fine. I think we're all feeling the effects of what's happened."

"No, it's not fine. Please hear me out," she insists. "I actually have a confession to make. I've done something terrible."

Confession? Admittedly, my brain immediately goes to Peyton's "accident." Hmm … now there's a thought. *Could Belinda have caused her accident?* Maybe they were arguing and Peyton fell?

"A confession?" I ask, clearing my throat. I try to subtly reach for my phone. "What about?"

She puts her head back and takes a deep breath like she's about to reveal a deep dark secret. "After Joelle got fired and you took her place, I went behind your back and tried to sabotage you. I really wanted the director job, and I was upset and jealous." She looks away. "I'm just tired of feeling like I'm not good enough."

I feel my body relax, and I put my phone back down on my desk. Okay, truthfully I'm not surprised by what she's telling me. I could sense she was bothered just by her body language and the snide comments she makes to me. What does surprise me is why she's admitting this to me now. Belinda's never been one to show any emotion, except when she's mentioned her son or her resemblance to Marilyn Monroe.

"Oh wow, for a second I thought you were going to confess that you accidentally pushed Peyton down the stairs," I say nervously.

Belinda looks appalled. "What? How could you say such a terrible thing? I would never."

"I know. I'm sorry," I say. "Anyway, why are you telling me this?"

She's still frowning at me as she folds her hands and places them in her lap. "I came to talk to you because I feel bad about how I acted. It's too late to apologize for the way I treated Peyton, but it's not too late to tell you that I'm sorry."

I'm trying to detect some sincerity, but it's difficult. Is she just saying this because Peyton's gone and now she's running the front desk solo? Or is she really feeling bad?

"I appreciate that," I say, tears pricking my eyes again. "I know you two didn't get along, but Peyton was my friend and a good employee."

My phone rings loudly, causing me to jump out of my seat. I look at the screen and see that it's Detective Cain.

"Excuse me, Belinda. I've been waiting on this call from the detective."

She raises her eyebrows as she stands up from the chair.

As soon as Belinda closes the door behind her, I tell Detective Cain that I found something in Alfie's office. I decide to leave out the specific details, just in case the walls of my office have grown ears. He asks me to meet him at the police station, and I couldn't be happier to get out of this hotel.

I grab my handbag and make the quick decision to exit through one of the side doors to avoid photographers and reporters. As soon as I get in my car, I see something out of the corner of my eye. I turn to look and think I see a figure turn the corner near the hotel entrance. Maybe my imagination is playing tricks on me, or maybe someone is watching me. This thought causes a shiver to shoot through my body so I quickly lock the door and start the car. I can't get out of this parking lot fast enough.

As soon as I arrive at the station, I tell the detective about the experience I just had in the parking lot. "I'm telling you, I think someone was there, watching me," I say, my voice shaking.

As usual, he jots a few things down on his notepad. "Did you notice anyone following you inside? Or see anyone around when you exited the building?" he asks.

I shrug. "I don't think so, but I wasn't really paying attention. I was focused on going through the side door to avoid the media."

What if someone *was* following me? I've been very vocal about searching for answers about Phoebe's death. The thought causes me to shudder.

"I can talk to Mr. Sheridan about keeping an officer on the premises, at least for the time being."

This makes me feel a little better, especially because I don't trust Alfie's security measures anymore.

"When I spoke to you earlier, you said you found something in the security office?"

What?

"Oh, yes, I was so distracted by the parking lot that I almost forgot why I'm here." I take the article out of my pocket and explain how I found it hidden under a desk calendar and stack of files in the security office. I also show him the text messages from Peyton.

"I already showed these to Ryan, but I thought you may also want to see them."

I watch his reaction as he reads them. "Interesting. We haven't been able to locate Ms. Fortier's phone yet."

He takes more notes as he reads through the article. "Do you know if Phoebe Phord had any kind of connection or relationship with Alfred Esposo?"

I shake my head. "None that I know of, but he was romantically involved with Peyton. Their relationship was just starting, so it wasn't common knowledge."

He continues to write in his notepad.

"When I talked to Alfie, he told me there wasn't any footage of Peyton's fall."

"That's correct."

"Which means someone could have tampered with the cameras in the east tower or erased the footage," I say.

"Yes. The camera angle switched, and but the time it flipped back to the staircase, Ms. Fortier was already at the bottom."

"So now there is no security footage at the time of either death."

"That's right. Unfortunately, we haven't been able to establish any connection between Mr. Esposo and Ms. Phord, yet. That's why I asked you if you knew of anything."

Ah—so they have been looking into this. I knew they weren't telling us everything about their investigation.

"I don't think so. They barely had any interaction, and she never mentioned him to me." I pause. "But couldn't it be possible that he's working with someone who did have a connection to her, maybe James? And I just happened to find an article about her on his desk. Isn't it possible that he got this from James?"

The corner of his mouth curls up. "Very good. Maybe you should go into police work."

I snort. "No, thanks. I just want to know what happened to my friends."

The thought of Alfie being involved, helping to cover up this horrendous crime. I can't even begin to wrap my head around this.

"This is definitely helpful," he says, holding up the magazine clipping. "Although, if he goes looking for it, he may suspect you took it."

I feel sick to my stomach.

"I will let our officers know that they need to keep a close watch on you," he says, his voice growing serious. "I would advise you not to exit the hotel alone."

The thought of poor Peyton comes to my mind. "So, do you think Peyton found out what happened to Phoebe, and someone wanted to keep her quiet?"

"It's a possibility. Unfortunately, we haven't located any witnesses yet."

I let out a frustrated growl. "How do you do this every day without losing your mind? It's so frustrating to not knowing what really happened and not being able to get justice for people."

He gives me a half smile. "It's tough. But once again, I assure you we're doing everything we can to get the answers we're looking for. You've really been a huge help. You should feel good about that."

Hmmm … I won't feel good until the person—or people—who killed my friends is brought to justice.

"I know you are … and remember, I will continue to help in any way I can."

Chapter Seventeen

*W*hen I check my phone after leaving the police station, I find two texts from Max asking me to call him. My stomach does a weird flutter when I see his name on my screen. One thing is for sure, I have to get a grip on these emotions I feel when it comes to Max. He's my boss!

"Maxwell Sheridan," he answers.

"Hi, Max. It's Casey Cooper." *Ugh, why did I just include my last name?* There's something about talking to this man that causes me to make a complete ass of myself. At least I haven't broken out into song since that first day in my office.

"Hello, Casey Cooper," he says, with a snicker.

"I just got your messages," I say, ignoring his teasing. "I'm actually just leaving the police station. I was meeting with Detective Cain."

"You were?" he asks, sounding surprised. "When I saw you

earlier, you were hell-bent on getting answers from Alfie. Did you find something?"

"I did, and hopefully it's helpful to the police. I'm sure you'll get the report later. Anyway, you asked me to call you?"

"Yes, I was wondering if you were planning on coming back to the hotel today," he says. "Or are you taking the remainder of the day off like you're supposed to?"

My stomach begins to twist at the thought of going back to the hotel right now, especially after feeling like someone was watching me in the parking lot. "Believe it or not, I was thinking about following your orders and heading home, unless you need me to come back. I know we still have a lot of work to get to."

He's quiet for a few seconds.

"Max, are you still there?"

"Yes, I'm here. Actually, I was going to ask if we could meet up to go over a few things, but I still think you need time away from the hotel. How about we meet at The Venti-Grand Café for coffee and have a quick meeting? But if you need to go home, I totally understand."

He wants to meet up with me … for coffee? I remind myself not to read too much into this. I have no reason to believe it's not perfectly innocent and professional to meet and drink coffee. I haven't had a coffee *meeting* in quite a while. This wouldn't be a big deal if Max didn't look like one of Marvel's future movie heroes.

"Sure, coffee sounds good. When?" I cringe. That sounded eager—*too* eager.

Thankfully he doesn't seem to notice, and we agree to meet at the café in thirty minutes. This will give me time to open my laptop and get my brain to switch away from detective mode and into customer relations mode. I really need to get my mind off missing packages, mysterious texts, and potential murders suspects. Throwing myself into my lengthy to-do list sounds like the best thing I can do right now.

When I arrive at The Venti-Grand Café, I order a skinny vanilla latte and sit down at a table in the corner. Thank goodness I brought my laptop with me during my mad dash to the police station. I open my computer, and I'm met with a reminder message from Judd Dawson's law office.

Phoebe's will reading has been looming over me since I was asked to attend. I have no idea what to expect, and honestly, I'm just hoping for some kind of message from her that will lead me to some answers. The anxiety of being named in her will is overwhelming, and after seeing James's reaction to me being invited to the reading, I expect some pushback from him—and maybe others—when we find out why Phoebe included me.

I look over my list of things I want to discuss with Max. I quickly add security and registration staff to my list. Thinking about this makes me feel like I've been punched in the stomach. Just knowing that Peyton will never be working with me at the hotel again is heartbreaking. The loss of her is going to be significant in more ways than one. Not only was she a friend, but she was a great employee. I close my eyes and try to take a few soothing breaths to keep from melting down.

When I open my eyes, I see Max walking toward me. He's loosened his tie, and his top button is undone. This is the first time I've seen him not looking so formal, and believe me, it's a welcome sight to behold.

I sit up straight in my chair. "Hey."

He sits down across from me. "Hi. Thanks for meeting. I almost called you back to cancel because I feel like a jerk for asking you to meet after I demanded you take time off."

I shrug my shoulders. "It's fine. I already told you that sitting at home alone isn't going to change anything for me. At least if I have a distraction, I won't be thinking about Phoebe and Peyton."

He runs his fingers through his hair. "I know. I figured by meeting here we could get some work done without all the distractions of the hotel." He sighs. "And there are a lot right now."

I finally notice how completely exhausted he looks. He has gray shadows below his eyes, and his hair is disheveled. This is a change from the first day I met him.

"Can I ask you something?"

He nods.

"Are you regretting your decision … taking the manager position at The Fountain Rose?"

He lets out a slow breath. "That's a good question, and I admit I've been struggling with some doubts," he says, clearing his throat. "Remember, this conversation doesn't leave this table."

I nod my head quickly. "Of course not."

"I've dealt with a lot in my career and, usually, I'm up for a good challenge."

"And by 'challenge,' you mean unruly guests, parties, maybe some theft …"

He snorts. "Yeah, something along those lines. Definitely not two deaths, including a legendary soap opera queen. It doesn't help that this has all happened since I arrived."

He loosens his tie a little more and continues talking. "I've turned some of the worst hotels into five-star destinations. I've been looking at the reports, and one of my biggest concerns right now is that the reservations department is showing a significant decrease each day since Phoebe's death. Frankly, it's extremely worrisome."

"I was wondering if this was going to happen," I tell him. "But I can understand why. It's scary to think that someone who was in the hotel that day could be capable of hurting another person. Despite the media's story that Phoebe killed herself, I think the public is smart enough to have doubts. Who's to say that someone else won't get hurt? Look at Peyton. In fact, I think someone was following me when I left the hotel earlier."

He gets a worried look on his face. "What do you mean?"

I recall the moment in the parking lot from earlier today. "When I left the hotel to go to the police station, I thought I saw a figure. I turned around and no one was there."

"Damn!" He pounds his fist on the table. "That's unacceptable! You shouldn't be afraid to come to work—none of our employees should be. And our guests need to feel safe during their stay with us." He stops and runs his fingers through his hair again. "I thought about what you said earlier, about the security cameras. Regardless if someone was tampering with them or not, we need to make massive changes immediately. I think it's time to upgrade the entire security system, new cameras, new technology. The current system is outdated anyway, practically ancient."

And we may need a new security staff.

"That's actually what I was talking to the detective about," I say. "I'm assuming you haven't spoken to him yet?"

He shakes his head. "I haven't. Should I be concerned?"

I tell him about the magazine clipping I found.

"Well, it's certainly looking like Alfie's up to his neck in all of this."

I make a face.

"What? Why are you making that face?"

I bite my lower lip. "I definitely think Alfie is involved. Two people died in our hotel and nothing was caught on camera." A shiver runs down my spine. "However, I feel like there's more to it. Like Alfie's only a small piece of the puzzle."

"If he tampered with the security cameras, erased footage, or turned them off so the crimes could be committed without a trace, that makes him more than a small piece of the puzzle," he replies.

I know he's right. I'm just having such a difficult time admitting the possibility that someone I thought was my friend would be involved in something so terrible. And what about Peyton? He really liked her, or so I thought.

"Anyway, the reading of Phoebe's will is in a few days. I'm hoping that sheds some more light on her situation, at least something that could lead us to some answers. I truly believe her assistant, James, has something to do with her death, despite him having an alibi."

"Did she ever tell you she was including you in her will?"

"Not a word," I say. "Honestly, I never wanted anything from her. I cared about her as a person, not because of her money. She had enough people in her life who tried to take advantage of her. I can tell you that James was not happy that she included me."

He puts his hands on the table and leans in toward me. I catch a whiff of his cologne. "How do you know?"

Admittedly, his scent makes me lose my train of thought for a few seconds. "Um—oh, her attorney approached me at the funeral and invited me to the reading. James was definitely surprised, and then I saw him talking to Phoebe's cousin, Raven, as I was leaving the church. He seemed to be really distraught about something, and this was shortly after we found out about the will reading."

Max cocks his head to the side. "Is this the same cousin who you invited to stay at the hotel?"

"Yes," I trail off. "She said she found another place to stay."

Hmmm ... maybe she's staying with James?

Max clears his throat. "Casey, I have to say that I'm so impressed by you. Most people would fall apart dealing with the events that have transpired over the past few weeks, but not you ... you're amazing."

I feel heat rise to my cheeks. I've never been great at accepting compliments to begin with, and one coming from Max makes me even more nervous. "Thank you," I say, looking down at my hands. When I look up, he's watching me intently. I study his structured jawline and notice his full lips. Gah, why does he have to be so attractive?

"I hope I didn't make you feel uncomfortable," he says. "It just feels good to be able to talk to someone without the formalities. I told you I've always run a tight ship at my hotels, and for the first time in my career, I feel like I can't get a grasp on this place. Every time I think I'm making some progress, something else happens."

"I can help you," I say. "This job is all I have. That's why I want to do whatever I can to help us through this. I'm not going to stand by and let The Fountain Rose fall apart. It means too much to me."

He smiles. "Good. Then we're going to continue to work with the police and get to the bottom of these tragedies together."

Together? That sounds good to me. Really good.

Chapter Eighteen

*Y*ou know that feeling when you walk into a room and you just know that people have been talking about you?

That's exactly how I feel when I arrive at the Judd Dawson Law Offices and find James and Raven already there. They're sitting next to each other, close enough so other people wouldn't be able to hear what they were talking about. They were obviously having a private conversation before I arrived because they both pull back as soon as they see me.

I say hello and sit down across from them. After we exchange pleasantries, silence falls upon the room. I make myself busy looking around the office and taking it all in. I pretend to study the pictures on the bookshelves, the artwork and framed college diplomas on the walls.

James and Raven are now both looking at their phones, no longer acknowledging each other. James is dressed in a navy-blue suit with a blue and white checkered dress shirt underneath it, no tie, and a matching pocket square. Raven is wearing a (very) low-cut, tight, light pink-colored dress. They both seem to be extra dressed up for the occasion. Of course, I'm also wearing a dress. Honestly, I had no clue on the appropriate attire for the reading of someone's last will and testament, so I Googled it.

"Good morning, everyone," Judd announces as he enters the room. "We're just waiting on one more person, and then we'll get started. Please help yourself to some coffee." He's not wearing a tuxedo today. Instead, he's wearing a salmon-colored sport coat with off-white pants and boat shoes. He looks like he has plans to go sailing on a yacht today. Who knows? Maybe he does.

None of us makes a move for coffee, and the painful silence continues.

I've been feeling anxious since the second I woke up this morning. I should've had a cup of tea. The truth is I don't want to be in Phoebe's will. She lived her life with people trying to take advantage of her, and I'm not one of them.

A few minutes later, a man I don't recognize with a blond ponytail walks in and sits down. He has bright green eyes and a bad spray tan.

He holds his hand out to shake mine. "Hallo, I'm Klaus. I'm—I was Phoebe's agent."

"I'm Casey Cooper. Phoebe was a dear friend, actually more like a sister to me."

"Ahh—yes, she spoke of you often."

Out of the corner of my eye, I notice Raven and James glance at each other. That's not obvious or anything.

Judd Dawson sits down at the end of the table and places a folder in front of him. He folds his hands and rests them on top of the folder. "Welcome, everyone. This is the reading of the last will and testament of Phoebe Phord, otherwise known as Phoebe Louise Fransen."

I try to swallow the lump in my throat. I sit up straight as Judd begins to read.

"Okay, here we go. I, Phoebe Phord née Fransen, publish and declare this document to be my last will and testament, and I revoke all former wills, codicils, and separate written lists, if any."

James groans and looks at Raven. I'm guessing he didn't like the part about revoking former wills.

First, Judd announces that to Klaus, Phoebe has left a vintage Steinway grand piano. *Wow, that's cool.* I glance at Klaus, who looks pleased.

"Marvelous, thank you," Klaus says, holding his hands up in the air. I'm not sure if he's talking to Judd or to Phoebe.

Judd continues, "To my assistant, James, I leave one hundred thousand dollars."

Damn. That's a lot of money—at least it is to me.

I watch James's face fall, as if he doesn't seem satisfied with that. Seriously, one hundred thousand dollars would be amazing. What an ungrateful ass.

Judd continues to read. "To my cousin, Raven, I leave Grandmother Willa's vintage Wedgwood china."

That's not a surprise, given the way she described their family's situation. Still, she seems shocked and appalled at the thought of family china.

Judd clears his throat before continuing. "I leave the remainder of my estate, including all accounts, assets, and my condo in Malibu to my adoptive sister and friend Casey Cooper."

A gasp escapes my mouth. There's no way I heard him correctly. I glance at James and Raven, and they both look as stunned as I feel.

"Um, there must be some mistake," I exclaim.

"I should think so," James adds.

"She's not even family," Raven snarls.

Judd looks down at the papers in his hands. "No, there's no mistake. Phoebe's wishes were made very clear."

I look at James and Raven who are now whispering to each other. This causes a stir inside me. "I thought you two didn't know each other," I say calmly. "You've certainly become fast friends."

Raven ignores me. "That's none of your business. And before you make any plans, you should know that I will be contesting this will. That estate belongs to my family. Scarlett and Phoebe took everything from Grandmother Willa and left my mother and me with nothing. I won't stand by and let some stranger take what's rightfully mine. You claim to be the sister Phoebe never had—we'll see about that. It's time that the world knows the type of person Phoebe Phord really was. I refuse to be silent any longer."

James holds out his hand to try to stop her but to no avail.

"She was selfish and hateful," she continues. "I wanted to be close to her, to have a relationship, but Scarlett tossed me aside. I'm not going to let her give everything that belongs to my family to some stranger. I'm going to get what's rightfully mine."

She rises to her feet and storms out with James at her heels.

Judd continues to read despite Raven's outburst.

I'm still trying to process what's happening. "You don't seem phased by that behavior," I say, pointing toward the door.

He shrugs. "She's not the first person to tear out of my office following the reading of a will. Money brings out the worst in a lot of people, especially in people that believe they're being cheated out of something they think they deserve." He hands me a sealed envelope. "Ms. Cooper, this is also for you."

I take the envelope from him, and I immediately recognize Phoebe's intricate handwriting. I remember a conversation we had when she told me her mother made her take calligraphy classes when she was younger. I don't move as I stare at the envelope in my hand.

"So, what happens now? If Raven's going to contest this, will I be dragged into court? I'm not sure I want to be a part of some lengthy legal battle. I'm not even sure I want any of it."

Judd purses his lips. "You have the right to disclaim this

inheritance. If you choose to do so, it will return to the estate. Ms. Phord also mentions some charitable organizations as an alternate, but again it was her wishes for you to receive the majority of her estate."

I look at the envelope. "Honestly, I'm in shock. Maybe this envelope contains something that will help make sense of this."

Judd takes off his glasses. "My advice to you would be to think about your options before making any decisions. And we can wait to see if Raven will continue with her contest."

I agree that I need some time to process this, but right now, I just want to get home and open this letter from Phoebe.

After leaving Judd's office, I practically sprint to my car. As tempting as it is, I don't want to open the envelope until I'm safely locked inside my house. I look at my phone to see I have a missed call from Detective Cain. I need to respond, but my mind is spinning. The first thing I want to do is get home and read Phoebe's letter. Hopefully it will explain why she decided to leave me almost everything she had.

When I'm safely curled up on my couch, the envelope clutched in my hands, I take a deep breath as I open it.

Chapter Nineteen

*A*s I read Phoebe's letter, the tears pour out of my eyes.

Dearest Casey,

I can only imagine how you're feeling at this very moment. You're wondering why I chose to leave the majority of my earthly possessions to you.

To answer your question—because I can. You know I like to do things my way, and this is the right thing to do.

After giving it more thought than you can imagine, I realized there isn't another person in my life who's as worthy of any of this as you are. This is a hard realization a person without a family must face.

By now, you may have met my cousin, Raven. I know I never told you about her, but we never had a relationship, so there wasn't much to tell. It wasn't for her lack of trying, and maybe I could have given her a chance. But I knew she was just like her mother and intent on latching on and bleeding me dry. There's a lot of dirty family water under the bridge and years of resentment that runs deep, from before Raven or I were ever born. I hope I'm able to put the rumors of our family secrets to rest before you're reading this. If not, just know that those rumors are not true, and I am working on getting the proof to back this up.

Thank you for being my friend, for listening to me when no one else would. Thank you for your sincerity and kindness. I know the challenges you've faced, similar to that of my own. Our lack of family and struggles with loneliness is what bonded us together in friendship.

Thank you for the beautiful bracelet. I know you didn't think I would wear it because it's not an expensive piece, but to me, it is priceless.

I was in the depths of despair when I met you following my husband's sudden death. I was able to let go of some of that anger because I had a friend, a true friend.

Thank you, Casey. I know these things are only monetary, but this is all I have to offer. I know you will put it to good use, and that's what I'm counting on.

Love, Phoebe

I wipe my eyes. Wow. So, out of everyone in her life, she chose me. Not her agent, her assistant, and certainly not her cousin. And she mentioned the bracelet. I really believe now, more than ever, that she dropped it on the floor for a reason. That's why I have to find out what happened to her.

I read over the part about the family rumors. I'm not clear on what she's referring to other than Raven's story about why they didn't have a relationship. Her claims about Phoebe's mother are completely the opposite of the way Phoebe described Scarlett to me. And what proof is she referring to? I feel like I need to show this letter to the detective. Maybe this will connect Raven to Phoebe's death.

I suddenly remember I have a missed call from Detective Cain. I try calling him back, but he doesn't answer, so I leave a message.

"Hi, Detective. It's Casey Cooper, returning your call. I have something to show you that I think will help with Phoebe's case. I'm going to bring it to the police station this afternoon."

I hear the front door open.

"Casey?" Kendall exclaims.

I dab the corner of my eyes.

"Hey, did you—" She stops and looks at me. "Oh no, what happened?"

I sniff. "I was just reading something."

"I guess you heard the news about Phoebe's cousin, or whoever she is."

My heart sinks. I'm afraid to ask because every time I turn around, I hear bad news. "What do you mean? Is this about Phoebe's will?"

She opens her laptop. "You don't know? She did an interview. She's now claiming that she's actually Phoebe Phord's sister and is contesting her will."

"Her sister?" I shout. *So that's what Raven meant by the snide comment she made about sisters during her outburst.*

"Apparently, she wasn't going to do this interview until she knew the contents of Phoebe's will. She claims she wasn't trying to tarnish Phoebe's reputation, but after being left out of the will, she felt the need to come forward and tell her story."

Hmmm … I don't believe she cared about Phoebe's reputation at all, especially because she said Phoebe supposedly shunned her.

Kendall continues, "She's claiming Phoebe's mother, Scarlett, gave her up when she was a baby, and her sister adopted Raven and raised her as her own. She said Phoebe's mother was so obsessed with Phoebe, who was a teenager at the time, and her own career, she didn't have time for another child."

My mouth drops open. "That can't be true."

I take the laptop out of Kendall's hands and read the article. Raven claims that she tried to reach out to Phoebe throughout her life, and Phoebe would never acknowledge her. Then on her deathbed, Raven's mother told her that she was actually Scarlett's child.

I look at Phoebe's letter that's still lying next to me on the couch. In the letter, she did say she hoped she would be able to clear up family rumors—obviously she died before she was able to do this.

Wait, that could be it. Maybe she did have the proof that Raven wasn't her sister? James and Raven seem too close to have just met, so what if they've known each other for a while? What if they cooked up this plan to get Phoebe's money, and James got a job as Phoebe's assistant to get close to her? Did they think one of them was likely to inherit her fortune? Did they kill her to get the inheritance now? It's totally possible, and that would explain why James seemed upset about me being at the will reading. Did I get in the way of their plan?

I must be zoning out because Kendall is waving her hand in front of me.

"Sorry. I was just thinking." I jump up from the couch. "I have to get to the police station."

～

I'm back in Detective Cain's office, waiting to talk to him about my theories. I'm holding Phoebe's letter tightly in my grasp.

"Ms. Cooper, thanks for coming in. I wanted to let you know that we were able to get the origin for the package that was taken from Ms. Phord's suite. We're still waiting on the information about its contents, but we do know it came from a lab."

"A lab? You mean like a medical lab?" OMG, that has to be the proof Phoebe had. "I think I may know what was in the package!" I exclaim, as I practically shove the letter at him.

He reads her letter slowly.

"Did you hear that Raven is now claiming she's really Phoebe's sister? Both she and James were furious that Phoebe left her money to me. I had a feeling that James and Raven knew each other better than two people who just met."

He slowly nods his head. "This is very helpful. But we still don't have proof that she was at the hotel, and he has a confirmed alibi."

I scratch my head. "I keep coming back to that. You said he was with family, which got me thinking about something. Phoebe had told me James didn't have any family. I actually think he may have been lying to her so he could manipulate his way into her life."

Detective Cain listens intently.

"What if someone pretended to be a family member, verified his alibi, and he did come to the hotel? Maybe Alfie tampered with the cameras so there was no trace of Raven and James being there, and Alfie still could have removed the package from the room. He did come into the room after me, and I was so distraught I wouldn't have noticed him taking the package. He also could have gotten the article about Phoebe from James." I pause and slowly exhale.

I still don't know why Alfie would be involved in Phoebe's death though, other than money.

"Well done, Ms. Cooper. This is great. I will get on all of this right away."

I nod. "I just want this to be over."

He smiles. "We're even closer to finding the truth now because of you."

"And what about Peyton?"

"Well, that's tough because we have no witnesses. But taking into account that there is once again no security footage and the texts she sent you, we're treating it as a potential homicide."

My face falls. "Even though I suspected she didn't trip by accident, it's still difficult to hear that someone could've intentionally wanted to hurt her."

He nods. "I know. In the meantime, we will continue to do everything we can to get to the bottom of this."

When I arrive at the hotel two days after my conversation with Detective Cain, things seem to have calmed down. The lobby isn't as chaotic, and it almost feels like business as usual. Most of the relentless photographers have moved on to harass other people.

I'm sitting in my office when Max appears in my doorway. "Hi. Welcome back."

I give him a half smile. "Thanks. You were right about me taking time off."

He gives me a smug look. "I told you."

I roll my eyes. "You love being right, don't you?"

He shrugs and sits down in the chair across from my desk. "Sometimes."

I giggle.

"I heard you talked to Detective Cain. It sounds like you've presented some really good information and theories."

I shrug. "I told you I was going to do everything I could to help them."

"Yes, you did." He pauses and scratches his forehead. "Casey, I hate to bring this up, but I wanted to let you know that I spoke with Peyton's family yesterday."

My smile fades. "Oh, you did? How did that go?"

He sighs. "They're devastated, of course."

I put my hand to my forehead. "I can't even imagine." I'm completely heartbroken for her family. Max tells me they're planning a service in her home town up north.

"The police have been in touch with them, and they know that her death is part of a bigger investigation."

I groan. "It never ends, does it?"

He shakes his head. "It sure seems that way."

We're both quiet for a few seconds when my phone rings. "Casey Cooper," I answer.

"It's about time!" Mikenzie's shrill voice yells into the phone.

I hold the phone away from my ear, and Max raises his eyebrows. "Hello, Mikenzie."

"I've been trying to get in touch with you, but your damn staff refused to give me your cell number. You know I was trying to give you a chance, but I'm extremely disappointed with the way I've been treated. Jojo would've never stood for this."

Max leans in to listen, so I put the speaker phone on. "You're absolutely right," I agree. "Unfortunately, with everything that's been happening around here, we aren't performing at our usual level of service."

"Well, you said it."

Max folds his arms and watches me intently.

Now is my time to shine. I need to show him why I deserve to be in this position. "Of course, that's not an excuse. You're one of our most important guests, so I would like to make it up to you."

I look at Max, and he gives me a thumbs up.

"That would be nice. But that's not what I wanted to talk to you about."

Oh no, I mouth to Max. I'm scared to ask.

"It has to do with the girl who fell down the stairs," she says.

My jaw drops open, and Max motions for me to get her to continue. "Peyton? What about her?" She's quiet for a few seconds. "Are you still there?"

"I would rather talk to you in person."

Max nods his head.

"Yes, absolutely. You're welcome to come to my office any time today."

She agrees to meet me later. Apparently, she has *several* appointments on her schedule. In other words, she's probably at a spa somewhere.

"What do you think that's about?" I ask Max as soon as I hang up.

He slowly shakes his head. "She definitely sounded serious."

I give him a thoughtful look. "I agree, but that doesn't necessarily mean anything. She's really dramatic. You should've seen the production she put on at Phoebe's funeral. She walked in on the arm of a friend and was completely sobbing. You would have thought she and Phoebe were inseparable."

"What kind of relationship did they have?"

I snort. "That's the thing. They didn't have one."

When Max leaves, I think about Mikenzie and all the odd interactions I've had with her. Both she and her friend were there when Phoebe asked about that package. One of them could've easily slipped in during the commotion and took it. Again, without any security footage, we continue to run into these barriers. And it's completely possible they took it just to find out what it contained. Them taking the package is certainly not out of the realm of possibility.

Chapter Twenty

A few hours later, I get a text from Mikenzie that she's on her way. I message Max to give him a heads up, but only because he asked me to. I really don't think it's necessary for him to be present when I talk to her, although I do feel an overwhelming sense of comfort when he's around.

Just when I'm about to give up on Mikenzie, Belinda pops her head into my office.

"Ruby Carson is here to see you," she says, rolling her eyes. "Everything is an emergency to that girl."

I bite my lip to keep from agreeing with her. *Our guests mean the world to us*, I remind myself. "You can bring her back," I tell her. Better late than never, I guess. And Belinda's right. For someone who makes everything seem like an emergency, she's taken her sweet time.

I let out an unexpected gasp when Mikenzie enters my office. She's wearing huge sunglasses, but they're not hiding that fact that every inch of her face is covered in bright red blotches. I knew she was getting some kind of spa treatment.

"Oh my, are you okay?" I ask pointing to my face.

"Oh, this?" she asks, waving her hand around her face. "Of course. I just had a laser treatment. Have you ever had one? It really helps with dull skin and fine lines. You should go to my girl. She's a miracle worker."

I ignore her obvious implication that I need to get laser skin treatment as I try not to stare, but her face looks like it's on fire.

Belinda is still lingering in my doorway. I thank her and ask her to close the door.

She looks at Mikenzie one last time before leaving. Not that I blame her, Mikenzie and her red face are quite a sight to behold.

"So, you said on the phone that you wanted to tell me something about Peyton?" I cut right to the chase, otherwise we'll be here all day discussing skin treatments.

"Peyton, right. I couldn't remember her name. I only dealt with Jojo, before you took over, that is."

Seriously, when is she going to get over my promotion? And I would think she knows Peyton's name by now, right?

"It was a very strange encounter, honestly. She was usually very efficient and attentive, and although I didn't deal with her on a day-to-day basis, she was polite and respectful when we had interaction. I appreciated how careful she was to call me by my alias, especially when other guests were present. I never saw her act that way before."

"What do you mean? How was she acting?" I ask.

Mikenzie gets a very serious look on her face.

I remind myself to take anything she says with a grain of salt. I'm not convinced I can trust more than half the things that come out of her mouth.

"Well, when I saw her the other day, she rushed by me and didn't even acknowledge me. At first, I was perturbed about it —I mean, what if I needed something? Especially because I heard you were taking a holiday."

A holiday? *Yeah, right.*

"I even called out to her, but she didn't respond. She was very distracted by something on her phone. And it almost looked like she was in a trance or maybe even on something. I mean, I'm not judging or anything, but she was supposed to be working."

I resist the urge to roll my eyes. Peyton didn't do drugs. "Did you see where she was going?" I ask.

Mikenzie gently touches her splotchy red face. "I actually followed her down the hall toward the east tower because I was concerned."

She was *concerned*? She didn't even remember her name.

"Did you hear her say anything?"

She purses her lips. "She was mumbling to herself about people not answering her calls. Whatever was on that phone was more important to her than the hotel guests. I want to make sure this isn't going to be a regular occurrence with your staff."

My heart sinks. *Was that when she was texting me?* Poor Peyton.

"Do you remember what time that was?"

She looks up thoughtfully. "I don't remember exactly. Maybe around eight thirty?"

I have to check my phone to see what time she texted me.

"Do you remember anything else?"

She glances at her phone. "I'm not sure. That's when my driver was texting me about being delayed in traffic. I was supposed to meet some friends for dinner, and I was terribly late. I was very frustrated, so I stopped following her."

Frustrated? *Like I am right now.*

"Why didn't you go to the police about this?"

She looks shocked. "The police? Why would I do that?"

I sigh as I try to come up with the right words. "Did you see her talking to anyone?"

Mikenzie narrows her eyebrows. "You don't think she fell down those stairs by accident, do you?"

I purse my lips. "I don't know what happened."

She stands up and puts her hands on her head. "Do you think someone purposely *pushed* her to her death? What the hell is happening in this hotel?"

I put my hands in prayer position as I attempt to calm her

down. "Nothing has been proven, but the authorities are investigating every possibility, as they should."

She starts dramatically pacing back and forth. "It's time for me to hire a bodyguard. I should have gone with my gut."

There's a knock on my door which causes her to stop her rambling.

"Come in," I call.

Max opens the door and smiles. "Hello, sorry to interrupt."

Mikenzie runs her eyes over Max, and I feel a spark of jealousy. *Hmmm ... that feeling can't be normal.*

"You're the new manager of the hotel," she says knowingly.

He gives her a nod. "Maxwell Sheridan. And you're Mikenzie Bronsyn, or is it Ruby Carson? We haven't officially met yet." I can tell he's trying not to stare at her red face.

"Yes, I'm Ruby Carson when I stay here. It's a necessity to have an alias when you're in the public eye on a daily basis."

Max presses his lips together and smiles.

"I'm glad you're here," she says. "I want to know what you're planning on doing to boost the security in this hotel."

Max gives me a look out of the corner of his eye.

"Ruby has been expressing her concerns about her safety while on the premises," I tell him in my most professional tone.

"You're damn right I am," she interrupts. "That front desk girl dies after falling down a flight of stairs, and now I hear the police are investigating whether it was an accident or not."

I give Max a helpless look. I have no room to say anything because I agree with her. I know these investigations have to go through the proper channels, but with every day that passes, someone is getting away with murder.

"We're working on updating our security system as we speak."

"It's too late for that. I'll be hiring my own security when I'm here," she says, grabbing her handbag. "I need to go put ice on my face, but I really hope you get things under control. You're going to lose a lot of business if people keep dying under this roof."

She's about to walk out when I stop her. "Please let me know if you remember anything else from the night you saw Peyton, and please consider telling the police what you told me."

She puts her huge glasses on. "I told you everything I saw, and I refuse to be dragged into your issues. You need to get this figured out, or I will be forced to find somewhere else to take my business."

As soon as she leaves, I let out a huge sigh. That wouldn't be such a bad thing. Just a few weeks ago, Peyton and I were talking about how great it would be if she stopped staying here.

"Well, that was mostly pointless," I tell Max.

"What happened to her face?"

"She did a skin treatment." I smirk.

He cringes. "That was scary."

I wince. "Yes, it was."

"And what did you want to tell me about Peyton?"

I tell him about our conversation, and the entire time, I'm wishing Mikenzie would've been paying more attention. She seemed more concerned with being ignored by Peyton than what happened to her.

"She freaked out when I asked if she talked to the police." I push my hair behind my ear. "She said Peyton looked like she was frantically trying to get in touch with someone. I'm wondering if that's when she was texting me." I grab my phone and scroll through my messages.

"Oh, no. She was trying to get in touch with me when Mikenzie saw her." I put my phone down on my desk. "Is this ever going to end?"

When I lift my head, Max is staring at me. "I'm sorry, Casey. I want this to be over as much as you do."

I nod. "I know."

"Have you eaten yet?"

I shake my head. "No, I haven't had much of an appetite in weeks."

"How about I order some food, and we can discuss the new security plans over dinner. I met with a new company today, and I was extremely impressed."

The sooner we up the security around here, the better I'll feel. "That sounds good."

Max goes back to his office to order from a local Mexican restaurant while I make my way to the front desk to check on registration.

Belinda raises her eyebrows and looks at me. I can't help but notice a gleam in her eye at the thought of me being caught up in a bunch of drama.

"So, Ruby Carson sure seemed to be desperate to speak to you. You two are awfully chummy."

I roll my eyes. "Hardly."

She shrugs. "It's okay. That's part of the job."

I groan under my breath. "Yes, it is."

Chapter Twenty-One

J stare at the food in front of me. I haven't taken one bite of the dinner that Max so generously ordered.

Max takes a sip from his water bottle. "Is something wrong with the food?"

I shake my head. "No, it's fine. I told you I haven't had much of an appetite."

My mind keeps going back to what Mikenzie said about Peyton. I feel so terrible about missing her texts. I wish I knew what she wanted to tell me. The more I think about it, the more I wonder if Alfie was working with James and Raven, and maybe Peyton found out about it.

"Has Detective Cain reached out to you yet?" I ask. "I'm just wondering if he has any new information. I really want James and Raven to pay if they did something to Phoebe."

"You don't know for sure that they're guilty."

"You're right. But it seems to me that they had the best motive. I just have to keep digging until I uncover the truth."

He tries to hide his smile behind his hand.

"What's so funny?" I ask. I don't let on that I'm irritated because I'm sure my job is already on thin ice. Blowing up at my boss isn't something I should add to my growing list of unacceptable workplace behavior.

"I wasn't laughing at you. I know how serious this is," he says with a serious expression. "Believe it or not, I'm actually in awe of you. The way you've handled everything that's happened—I know I've said it before, but I really mean it."

Okay … I wasn't expecting that. If anything, I was expecting a lecture on proper employee etiquette.

"I appreciate you saying that," I reply, swirling my water bottle around in my hand. "I've been feeling like I'm alone on the island."

He snickers. "You're definitely not alone."

I put the water bottle down on the table and nod. "Sometimes it feels that way."

Max grabs a notepad and pen from the middle of the conference table, flips open the pad, and clicks the pen. "Okay, so you think James and Raven could be guilty of killing Phoebe."

I nod. "Yes, I do. But according to the police, James has an airtight alibi. And even though James says he just contacted Raven after Phoebe died, I don't believe it. The way those two interact is not like two people who just met. I think it's very possible she was already in town, or she came to town when James contacted her. I'm even wondering if they've been together all along. Maybe before James started working for Phoebe. I think Raven knew she needed another way into Phoebe's life because Phoebe didn't want a relationship with her. Now she's claiming that her mother told her on her death bed that she's actually Phoebe's sister."

I watch as Max takes notes like he's a detective. I definitely don't mind working with him on this, and it helps to talk about this because I don't want to miss anything. I tell him about Phoebe's letter and about her wanting to get the proof to resolve family rumors.

"So, the package could've possibly contained the results that Raven was not her sister," he says.

I point my finger at him. "Yes. And that's where I think Alfie comes in. There's no security footage in the hotel that day, and he was one of the first people to join me in Phoebe's suite after I—" The unforgettable image of her staged body flashes through my mind once again, an image I know I'm never going to forget. "After I found her body on the floor. He could've removed the package. Or maybe someone else snuck in and grabbed it while he was with me. Either way, I wouldn't have known because I was so distraught. Detective Cain says the package was sent from a lab, and they are getting more information on what it contained. Also, he had that article about her in his office. I still don't understand why he would be involved, unless he was offered money to help. So, either he did it himself or he paved the way for someone to do it unseen."

He looks up from the paper. "So, you think he also pushed Peyton down those stairs?"

"I think it's a possibility. Mikenzie said that Peyton was not herself when she saw her that day. She said she was frantically trying to get in touch with someone. I think it's possible that she found out that Alfie was involved. Maybe she saw that article in his office and confronted him about it? He could have been trying to stop her and—"

My eyes begin to fill with tears, and I lower my head. A few seconds later, I feel a hand on my back. Without thinking I turn toward Max and fall into him. I continue to sob on his shoulder while he rubs my back very gently. I probably shouldn't be crying in my boss's arms, but right now, I have nowhere else to turn. And he's here, wanting to help and being so patient with me. Not to mention he's allowing me to keep my job despite my being a train wreck.

I pull away and quickly wipe my tears. "I can't continue to do this," I tell him. "Can we please talk about why we're here? Tell me about the—um—new security company."

Max stares at me. "You don't have to do this, Casey."

I clear my throat. "Yes, I do."

"Believe it or not, I can relate to how you're feeling. This wanting to throw everything you have into your career. How do you think I got here?"

I dab the corners of my eyes.

"I'm a workaholic, and my marriage ended because of it."

His *marriage*? Suddenly I want to know everything there is to know about this man. "How long ago was this?"

"I've been divorced for almost ten months, but our relationship ended long before that."

"I'm sorry."

He gives me a half smile. "Thanks. Unfortunately, my divorce only made things worse. I continued to work more and more, moved around to fix failing hotels because I couldn't fix my own life."

"Well, I hope you can fix this one."

"Me too. In fact, I really hope I do, because I think I want to stay here for a while. Maybe it's time to settle down."

My ears perk up at the mention of him settling down. I'm sure he means that he wants his life to settle down, not that he wants to *settle down*—as in, with a woman. Neither of us says anything for a few seconds.

"I'm glad you came here," I say finally. "Colton barely spoke to me when he was our manager. It wasn't just me either. He didn't bother with most of the employees. This is a nice change."

At what point do I need to stop talking? I don't want to cross any lines of professionalism, and the fact that I feel so drawn to Max can't be good. I certainly don't want a repeat of Colton and Joelle. Unlike my predecessor, I care about my job way too much to let a silly crush get in the way of my future career path. *But is this a silly crush? Or am I really falling for this man?* So, he makes me feel safe when it seems like everything around me is crashing down.

That's not enough to completely abandon my common sense, is it?

Max is watching me carefully while I give myself my internal pep talk.

"You okay?" he asks.

I nod absently. "Yeah, I was just thinking."

He laughs. "Be careful with that."

You have no idea.

Silence falls over the room again. It's not awkward. I just feel like I want to say something. "Max."

"Casey," he says at the same time.

We both laugh.

"Go ahead," I tell him.

The room gets so quiet that when he rubs his chin, I can hear his fingers brush across his five o'clock shadow. "I'm about to say something that I shouldn't be saying," he says.

I nervously chew on my lip.

We're interrupted by the sound of Max's phone. He looks resentfully at it.

"You should answer that. It could be important."

He lets out a low groan and reaches for it. "Okay, I'll be right there," he says a few seconds later.

Obviously our conversation is over, so I quickly pack up my untouched food.

"Can we finish talking later?" he asks.

I nod. "Sure. I should probably go home anyway. I'm exhausted."

I notice the police officer keeping an eye on me as I exit the hotel. I definitely feel safer knowing he's standing there protecting me. I just wish there was someone around who could protect me from my heart. I never thought this would happen to me, but it is. I'm falling for my boss, and I don't know what to do about it.

Chapter Twenty-Two

As soon as I arrive home, I grab a bag of Oreos, sit on the couch, and call my best friend. "Please tell me I'm making a huge mistake," I beg after telling her about Max and my growing attraction to him.

"Why would I do that?" she asks. "There's no rule that says you can't be attracted to him."

"Jenn, he's my boss," I exclaim. "I think you're forgetting how I got this job in the first place."

"Oh, stop," she scolds. "First of all, your old manager was married. And it's not like you and this Max guy are hooking up all over the hotel or engaging in illicit behavior."

That's true. We haven't acted on anything, yet. He was about to say something before we were interrupted. No matter how hard I try, I can't deny that there's a major connection between us.

My phone beeps. When I see Max is calling, my heart starts to race. I hurry Jenn off the phone to answer his call.

"I just wanted to check on you," he says.

A feeling of excitement comes over me. "I'm fine, just tired."

"I'm sorry we were interrupted earlier, I really wanted to finish that conversation."

"Yeah, me too …"

We're both quiet. Is he waiting for me to say something else? What the hell, I have nothing to lose at this point.

"What did you want to tell me?"

I hear him clear his throat. "Well, since you asked, I was going to tell you that I really enjoy working with you. With everything that's happened since the day I arrived at The Fountain Rose, the only good thing has been working with you."

Thankfully I'm sitting down because my knees have gone weak.

"I enjoy working with you too," I tell him. I toss the Oreos aside and start chewing on my thumbnail.

"I know things are complicated right now, and the last thing either of us needs is to draw more attention to the hotel."

"I agree," I interject.

"But I like to be very straightforward and honest. I don't have time to play around, and frankly, from the second you sang the hotel slogan, I knew I liked you."

I can feel my cheeks get hot. I'm so glad we're having this conversation over the phone. "Please don't remind me about that," I whine.

He laughs. "Hopefully, we can get all these issues resolved very soon. For now, let's just take things one day at a time."

"I'd like that." I should say something else, but I like where this conversation is going. If I open my mouth, another embarrassing song may fall out.

"I'm glad to hear that," he says.

"And I'm very ready to go back to running our hotel," I say, reminding him that I'm still one thousand percent committed to restoring our hotel to its former glory.

"Me too."

Our conversation quickly shifts to work, and I get the feeling that someone else is around. After getting off the phone, I call Jenn back and tell her all about my conversation with Max. I continue talking to her while I draw a hot bath. Maybe I can soak all my stress away?

As I lie in the hot bath water, I imagine being able to go to the hotel without police or photographers all over the place. I can't wait to work with Max and really get to know him better without a murder investigation hovering over us. I still don't know much about him other than he's divorced and now he's married to his career.

There's also a little voice inside me that's telling me to proceed with caution. Because if things do progress and then go south, it could affect my job. There's also the worry that he's too good to be true. He's handsome, successful, patient, and supportive—all qualities that any woman would want. So, maybe the only catch is that he's a workaholic. There are worse things.

~

When I arrive at the hotel the next day, my heart sinks. The shark photographers have returned, and there are police everywhere. I hurry inside to find out what happened, and I immediately notice Max and Detective Cain talking. Even Belinda, who is normally cool and calm, is looking a little overwhelmed while talking to guests.

"What happened?" I ask worriedly.

Max puts his hand on my shoulder but I'm so flustered that it doesn't even phase me.

"Alfie has been arrested," he tells me.

I feel both relieved and uneasy. "What did they find?"

"Our team discovered that the security cameras were purposely tampered with. He's been taken in for questioning," Detective Cain says, looking at his phone.

"So, he was involved with Phoebe's death? I knew it!" I exclaim.

Max and the detective exchange a look. "I'm actually referring to the cameras in the east tower," Cain says.

I frown. "You mean where Peyton died?"

He nods.

The very familiar feeling of nausea takes over my body. I

think about all the times Peyton would talk to me about Alfie, and I actually encouraged her to pursue him. Ugh. How could I be so wrong?

"Do you think he pushed her?" I ask, gritting my teeth.

"We aren't sure yet, but someone went to a lot of trouble to hide the truth about her fall."

"I'm glad things are finally moving along," I say, my voice shaking. "I want life to go back to normal. I want to move on." I catch a glimpse of Max who gives me an encouraging smile. I already know he feels the same way.

"We're getting closer to uncovering the truth," Detective Cain says. "You've been very helpful, Ms. Cooper—and we appreciate that."

"I want justice for my friends."

"They'll get it. I will make sure of it," he insists. "If you'll excuse me now, I have to get to the station."

He leaves Max and me alone.

"This is good news, right?" he asks.

I blow out a puff of air. "I hope so. Unless Alfie manages to get himself out of this somehow."

A few guests approach us, and we abandon our conversation. I check in with Belinda who's efficiently running the registration desk. Now if only I can concentrate on my job.

Chapter Twenty-Three

a few hours later, there's still no word on Alfie. I'm on the edge of my seat every time my phone rings. It's been a busy morning. I've taken care of complaint calls ranging from room service delivery times to noisy guests. I even received a call with a request to have guest room furniture rearranged because the current setup didn't spark good energy. Seriously? I couldn't make this stuff up even if I wanted to.

After a few more hours, I feel the need to get some fresh air and to pick up a late lunch, so I decide to take a walk to a café that's five blocks away. I think a break will do me some good. I take my time on my way, and as soon as I walk inside, I run straight into someone I wasn't expecting to see.

"Joelle?"

She looks as surprised as I feel. Honestly, I really thought she skipped town, or someone made her leave town after her sordid affair with Colton was revealed.

"Hello, Casey."

I try not to stare at her face, but she looks different. She's cut and colored her hair to a lighter shade of blonde. Her lips are noticeably fuller, and her cheekbones are more defined. I wonder if she did all of this on purpose. Obviously, she's been lying low, and I can't blame her.

"How are you doing?"

She stands up straighter and juts her chin out. "I'm great, actually, never been better. You?"

Before I can answer her, she continues talking. "I've been following everything that's going on at the hotel. I can't believe Peyton is gone. She was such a nice girl."

Joelle worked at The Fountain Rose for a long time, and she knew Alfie long before I ever did. Maybe she can enlighten me with some information about him.

"I know. It's been devastating," I tell her. "Especially right on the heels of Phoebe's death."

She gives me a sympathetic look.

"Oh, that's right. I remember you two were close. I didn't know her well because she rarely responded to me when I reached out to her. I finally just gave up on trying after she blew me off a few times."

I give her a tight-lipped smile. What she actually means is she gave up on the job completely. Her days (and nights) at the hotel were filled with partying and sneaking around with Colton. The needs of the guests weren't very high on her priority list, except for when it came to who she was hanging out with at the time.

"Congrats to you, though. How's the job treating you so far?"

I try to hide my shock that she asked me about the job. *Her old job.*

"Don't look so surprised. I know they promoted you after I left."

An imaginary lightbulb goes off in my head.

"Let me guess, Mikenzie told you. I don't think she believes I'm the right person for the job. She really misses you, *Jojo.*"

She shrugs. "I still don't understand why it was such an issue that Mikenzie and I were good friends. You and Phoebe were close. Good relationships with our guests are very important. It creates loyalty, and that's what will keep them returning."

Her idea of good relationships differs quite a bit from mine, but I don't say that out loud.

"I also heard that Maxwell Sheridan is your new manager. Better watch out for that one."

My pulse speeds up at the mention of Max. I have to find out what she means without raising any red flags.

"How do you know Max Sheridan?"

She gives me a wistful look that makes me nervous. "I actually never met him in person," she says. Relief immediately washes over me. "But I've heard stories. Is he as good-looking in person as he is in pictures?"

I shift from one foot to the other. "Yeah, I guess so," I say nonchalantly.

"What's he like to work for? I heard he's an arrogant ass, but apparently, the ladies still fall for him. One of those men who knows all the right things to say."

I don't know which ladies she's referring to, but that's not something I want to hear.

I shrug my shoulders. "He's been fine so far. Although, we haven't exactly been in a normal working environment. With the deaths of Phoebe Phord and Peyton, it's been complete chaos since he arrived."

"Whew, I'm glad I'm not there anymore."

As much as I want to know everything there is to know about Max, I want to ask her about Alfie. I clear my throat. "I do have a question. Did you have a good relationship with Alfie when you were at the hotel?"

She nods quickly. "Sure. Alfie was cool. Is it true that they arrested him?"

I press my lips together tightly. "He was taken in for questioning this morning. He's definitely been off lately, but I just assumed it was because of what's been happening at the hotel. He's been under a lot of pressure because of security issues, and now with Peyton gone ... I'm not sure if you knew this, but they had been seeing each other for a while."

She frowns. "Alfie and Peyton weren't dating."

I cock my head to the side. "Yeah, they were. I mean, they were keeping it quiet because—"

Damn. Way to stick that foot in your mouth again, Casey. I manage to stop talking before I mention her affair with Colton.

"Hmm … well, I guess he broke up with his girlfriend then," she says, shrugging.

Girlfriend?

"Alfie has a girlfriend?"

"Yeah, he has for quite a while, a year maybe? This is some juicy gossip," she says, leaning in closer to me. "She's an older woman, quite a bit older than him. He told Colton about her, but for some reason, there was some kind of secrecy behind it. I don't know much other than that. He just said he really loved her, but they had to keep their relationship hidden."

Huh?

"Oh, I had no idea," I reply, trying to sound like I don't care. But inside, I'm fuming. Why was he involved with Peyton if he had a girlfriend? He had us all fooled.

She takes a sip of her coffee. "I don't think anyone knew except for Colton. Anyway, maybe things ended with this other woman if he was seeing Peyton."

Or he was playing her along with the rest of us.

I nod slowly. "I guess so."

"Listen, please take care of Mikenzie," she says, changing the subject. "She's a good friend and loyal customer. She's brought the hotel a lot of business."

"Of course." I clear my throat. "I had no idea she was so close to Phoebe. She was one of the few people who attended her funeral."

Joelle waves her hand at me. "You know how those celebrities are. They all run in the same circles."

Joelle must be one of the few people who still considers Mikenzie a celebrity. I don't say that out loud. Instead, I nod in agreement.

She looks at her phone. "I need to go, but it was nice running into you."

"Yes, same to you."

"And good luck with everything over there," she calls over her shoulder. I watch as she takes off down the street. I hop in line to order my food, but I'm no longer hungry. My mind is replaying everything she told me—the stuff about Max and, of course, Alfie.

I'm so confused about Alfie. Was he just playing Peyton, and if so, why? Maybe he was only with her to cover up this secret life he had? Why would he have to keep his relationship a secret, and who is this mystery woman?

"Excuse me? Are you ready to order?" The girl at the counter drags me out of my daydream.

I absently order a turkey panini and a Diet Coke, but I'm still thinking about Alfie. I can't help but wonder how this is all connected, and what if Phoebe was this older woman? What if in some strange twist Phoebe and Alfie were closer than I ever knew. At this point, nothing would surprise me. I didn't know Raven existed, and I didn't have any inclination that Phoebe had plans to leave me everything she had. Maybe Alfie was with her to get his hands on her money. It wouldn't shock me because I've thought that money has been the main reason for her murder. This could explain a link between Alfie, James, and Raven, if my theories are correct. This could also explain why he had that article about her in his office.

Poor Peyton could have been in the wrong place at the wrong time and gotten caught in the crossfire.

I need to inform Detective Cain about this new information. Hopefully, it's what they need to finally connect Alfie to Phoebe's death.

I really want to talk to Max about this, but my thoughts switch to what Joelle told me about him. She told me I should stay away from him, but her warning could be baseless. From the day he showed up, he never made it a secret that he was difficult to work for. And what did she mean when she said the ladies always fall for him? Again, that could be more rumors. Joelle isn't the most trustworthy of people. I refuse to let her get inside my head. I've got bigger issues to worry about.

Chapter Twenty-Four

*W*hen I return to the hotel, I lock myself in my office, return a few emails, and call Detective Cain. I tell him about my conversation with Joelle, and once again, he thanks me for being helpful.

After I'm off the phone, I begin to make a list of everything that's happened with Alfie since the day Phoebe died. We know there was no security footage that day. Alfie was insistent on being present when James wanted to have a private conversation with me right after Phoebe died. He could have been worried about James slipping up and revealing something important.

I stare at my paper and feel like there are pieces missing. Seeing Joelle definitely filled in some of the gaps, but so many questions are running through my mind right now. What did Peyton want to tell me? Could she have found out about Alfie's girlfriend? And could it really be Phoebe? Or maybe she found evidence that Alfie tampered with the security system the day of Phoebe's death?

I reach for my office phone and dial Max's extension. He's the only person I can talk to about this right now.

"Max Sheridan," he answers. I can tell he has me on speaker phone, so I'm careful to sounds as professional as possible.

"Hey, Max. It's Casey. I wanted to discuss a few things with you before you leave today. It will only take a few minutes. Can you let me know when you're available?"

"Sure. I'll be over there in a few."

"Thanks so much." I quickly hang up and release the breath I was holding in.

I look at my notes. There's something else missing. Hopefully Max will be able to help.

My office phone rings, and I answer right away.

"This is Casey."

"Hi, girl, it's Mikenzie. I wanted to inform you that I will be there this weekend with my two very best friends. We need to make all the arrangements in advance, just in case you decide to take off again."

I roll my eyes while I listen to her newest list of endless demands. Her most recent requests include brand-new down pillows, the fridge fully stocked with coconut water, and salt lamps placed throughout the suite.

Sigh. It must be nice to only worry about things like what to have waiting for you in your luxury hotel suite.

I let her know I will have everything ready for her when she arrives. The truth is, as annoying as she can be, I'm happy to be working and not thinking about everything else.

As soon as I finish making all the arrangements, Max pops his head into my office.

"Sorry it took me so long. I've been working with the new security company all day. Chuck seems to be handling things really well in Alfie's absence, but I'm thinking we need to hire a whole new team once the new equipment is in place." He sits down across from me. "So, what's up?"

I fold my hands and spin around in my chair. "I had an interesting run-in today."

He raises his eyebrows. "Oh, yeah? With whom?"

I tell him about my conversation with Joelle, carefully leaving out any mention of him. He's on the edge of his seat when I tell him about Alfie's secret relationship and my theory on who it could be.

"You think it was Phoebe?" he interrupts.

I throw my hands into the air. "I think it's very possible. He did have an article about her in his office. Maybe he was involved with her for her money? This is where James comes in. He had access to everything in her life, and Alfie had access to the security of this hotel. It totally makes sense that they could've been working together all along."

"Huh. Good point."

I slide the list I made across the desk to him. "I was making some notes, trying to tie Alfie to everything. What do you think?"

I chew on my lip while I watch him read. Damn, he has gorgeous eyelashes. That's so not fair. I'd have to put out a lot of cash to get those lashes.

"Casey?"

Oh, hell. How long has he been talking to me while I was admiring his features?

"Sorry, I zoned out."

"I was saying that we should call Detective Cain. If Alfie and Phoebe were having a secret relationship, that could be the motive they've been searching for."

"I already spoke to him."

He smiles. "I should've known. You're amazing."

His compliment causes heat to fill my cheeks.

"I'm sure you're wanting to get home and get a break from all the madness," I say, trying to change the subject.

He shakes his head. "Not really. I don't even have my TV set up yet. Sadly, I'm still living out of suitcases and boxes. Every day, I tell myself I'm going to unpack, but I've just been avoiding it."

"*You* might need to take some time off *yourself*," I tell him.

He laughs. "Me? Take time off? Not likely. Like I said, work is my life."

"What about friends?"

He shakes his head. "I haven't had time to venture out yet. Most of my good friends are still back home in the Bay Area.

I've moved around way too much to make lasting relationships since then."

That's sad.

"How about you?"

I tell him about Jenn and Kendall. Phoebe was the only other person I was really close to.

"I'm terrible at keeping in touch. I have all those social media pages, but I rarely go on there. Sometimes it's difficult to see people moving on with their lives, having successful careers, getting married, having kids ..." I stop talking. Wow, I sound pathetic.

"I know exactly what you mean."

I give him a grateful look. "Sorry. I sound like such a downer."

He shakes his head. "You're being honest."

We continue to exchange a few glances without saying anything. His eyelashes, his lips, his shoulders ... gah! I jump up from my chair before I start drooling all over the desk.

"Are you done for today?" he asks, clearly noticing my sudden movement.

"I sure am."

"Do you want me to walk you out?"

I give him a grateful smile. "That would be good, thanks."

Max goes to his office to collect his things, and I stop by the registration desk. The lobby is quiet, and Belinda is scrolling through her phone. She gives me a smug look and puts her phone down. She definitely seems calmer than she did when I first arrived this morning.

I sigh because I already know what she's thinking. In my defense, it's my job to interact with our hotel manager.

"How did things go out here? Were you able to calm any guests' concerns?"

She rolls her eyes. "Silly girl, of course. All the guests that I've spoken with are content and happy."

"Great."

I shift from one foot to another. Maybe I should just leave without Max. What if people do get the wrong idea and start whispering?

"You're on the late shift tonight?" I ask.

Belinda starts carefully rearranging the floral bouquets that are adorning the counters.

"I sure am. I told Max I would fill in as much as possible until we hire more staff. Poor Sami is doing double duty with reservations."

I have to give her credit. She really does care about her job.

"Thanks, Belinda. I appreciate all your hard work. You really do care about this place. We should all put in as much effort as you do."

She turns and puts her hand on my shoulder. "Thank you. That truly means a lot coming from you."

I sense a hint (or more than a hint) of sarcasm in her voice.

"Casey, I know I told you I wasn't going to try to overstep my boundaries, but I feel like I should offer you some advice."

And here we go. I knew this was coming.

"I'd be very careful if I were you."

"I'm not clear on what you're referring to."

She purses her lips together and gazes behind me. I turn around to see Max talking to one of the police officers.

"Have you heard any news about Alfie?" she asks, changing the subject. Of course, she's not going to lecture me about Max when he's a few feet away.

I frown. "Not yet."

"I still can't believe they dragged him down to the police station. Good evening, Max." She quickly changes the subject when Max joins us.

"Belinda, thank you for your diligence with our guests today. You've really stepped up with everything that's been going on."

She flashes him a broad smile and playfully touches her platinum blonde hair. Hmmm …maybe Joelle was right about him saying all the right things. I do understand, though, that Max has a very commanding presence.

"Well, have a good night," I tell Belinda.

"I'm walking out too," Max says casually.

That was totally obvious, but if it doesn't bother Max, then it shouldn't bother me.

On our way out to the parking lot, we stay a few feet apart while Max loudly talks about ordering new pool loungers and umbrellas. He even stops to pick up a few stray pieces of paper. He is smooth, I'll give him that.

As we approach my car, he stops talking.

"Thanks for walking me out."

"I know I said we should take things slow, but do you want to go somewhere?" he whispers.

Oh, my gosh. Yes.

Okay, so admittedly, my mind starts going in a million different directions. Where exactly is he thinking? Dinner, his place, my place, Cabo? Seriously, the possibilities are endless.

"I do, but …" I clear my throat while doing a quick scan of the parking lot. Why do I always feel like I'm being watched? Maybe I'm just being paranoid because of what happened last time.

"But what?" he asks.

Everything inside me is screaming yes, but I feel like I need to tell him about Belinda. And Joelle's warning is still in the back of my mind.

"I think people are starting to talk."

He runs his hand through his hair. "Why, because we've had some meetings?"

I shrug. "I just think they pay attention to what's going on after what happened with Colton and Joelle."

He narrows his eyebrows. "Okay. How about coffee then? Tomorrow morning."

Coffee makes everything innocent.

"I'd really like that."

He moves a little closer to me, which causes my heart to beat a little faster. "There isn't anything wrong with us meeting for coffee, so people shouldn't talk about that," he says softly.

His voice soothes my nerves. Why does being around this man makes me feel so safe?

I swallow nervously as I open my door. "I know."

"I look forward to seeing you in the morning," he says softly.

"Me too."

He holds my door open for me, and I slide into my car. We both hesitate for a few seconds before he closes the door.

Now I only have a few hours to wait before seeing him again. Crap. I guess Joelle was right—he does know how to make the ladies fall.

Chapter Twenty-Five

After a night full of tossing and turning, I get out of bed and start my day. I'm just getting ready to leave when I get a text from Max canceling our coffee meeting. He apologizes but tells me he has to meet with the detective, and it's important. I'm hoping that means there's news about the case.

I admit I'm disappointed we won't be having "coffee" together, and now I wish I hadn't freaked out last night. It wouldn't have been a big deal to go to dinner with him, assuming that's what he was referring to when he asked if I wanted to go somewhere.

Kendall is making coffee when I walk into the kitchen. Somehow coffee with my roommate in my kitchen doesn't seem as enticing as spending time with Max.

"Morning. You're up early. What time did you get home last night?"

She rubs her eyes. "I don't even know. I came home to get a

few hours of sleep, and I barely remember getting here. We've been trying to make this deadline, and I'm completely exhausted. We filmed all day yesterday, and I have another full day ahead of me."

I grab a banana and sit down at the table.

"What's happening with you?" she asks over her shoulder. "How are things at the hotel? Any updates on the case?"

I sigh. "It seems like every day something pops up that throws me off. Just when I think I have things figured out, *bam*, something shocking happens. Our head of security, Alfie, was taken in for questioning yesterday. Even though I suspected there was more going on with him, it's still hard to accept that he could be involved in a murder plot."

She leans against the counter as she pours creamer into her coffee. "Trust me, I've been there. I can't tell you how many days I was afraid to go to the studio, fearing for my safety and possibly my life. And then when the phone calls and the threats started—well, you remember what happened. When you're in the middle of the chaos, it feels like there isn't an end in sight."

"That's how I feel right now," I tell her. "I want it all to be over, so I can get back to my regular boring life."

She giggles. "There's something to be said about a regular boring life."

"That's the truth." For some reason, the thought of a regular boring life makes Max pop into my head. I could get used to a regular life working side by side with him at the hotel. That would definitely make it easier to put up with

Mikenzie Bronsyn and all her crazy demands on a weekly basis.

"I need to get ready and get back to the studio," Kendall says, putting her cup in the sink. She gives me a curious look. "You sure you're okay? You know I'm here if you need me. I'm not kidding, I will tell my director I have an emergency if I have to."

I give her a grateful smile. "Thanks. I'm okay."

She hurries to her room, leaving me alone with my thoughts. It's a good feeling to know I have someone else to turn to if I need something. Kendall and I have been through a lot together. I'm realizing that I need to appreciate the friends I have here who have my back. This reminds me how much I miss Phoebe.

I quickly fix my makeup, brush my teeth, and head to the hotel. Hopefully today is the day we finally get some answers.

When I first started working at The Fountain Rose Resort, I was mesmerized by the gorgeous lobby, high-profile guests, and the novelty of such a luxurious place. It all seemed so exciting to me, and I truly believed I hit the jackpot of jobs. I still remember my first day like it was yesterday. Joelle took the time to walk me around and give me the lay of the land. I'm pretty sure that was long before she was involved with Colton because she seemed very dedicated and focused on doing the best she could at her job.

Needless to say, I haven't had that same feeling of excitement lately. Having two friends pass away in the hotel has hung a cloud of darkness and funk over The Fountain Rose Resort. I'm reminded that my dear friends are gone every day I'm here.

When I arrive this morning, there's definitely a weird vibe. Sami immediately pulls me aside and tells me that she heard Alfie has been named as the prime suspect in Peyton's accident.

"The article claims that Alfie panicked, so he got rid of all the video."

I cringe at the thought.

"It had to be an accident," she says. "Alfie wouldn't hurt Peyton on purpose, right?"

I ignore her question as a woman with the smallest dog I've ever seen approaches the desk.

"Good morning," I say cheerfully. "How can we help you?"

The woman requests a dog walker for her teacup puppy, Sir Mix A Lot. Yes, that's the name of her dog, and it takes every ounce of strength not to laugh. Which is a shame because I really could use a good laugh right now.

Believe it or not, we do have a dog walker on staff. This was actually something Joelle implemented, and many of our guests were ecstatic about it. It really was a genius idea. This is just one of the many ways our hotel is all about making our guests have the best experiences while they are with this. It would be a terrible shame for all the negative publicity to keep guests from staying here.

As soon as our guest and Sir Mix A Lot leave, Sami resumes talking about Alfie again.

I'm only half listening because I'm checking my phone. I texted Max earlier and still haven't heard back from him.

"No way!" Sami exclaims. "Twitter is blowing up right now. Look at this."

She shoves her phone at me, and I immediately see pictures of Raven and James. I scroll through and read the comments.

Based on an anonymous tip, police are also investigating both the assistant and cousin of Phoebe Phord in connection with her alleged suicide at The Fountain Rose Resort."

Anonymous tip? I wonder if they're referring to me. I wasn't exactly anonymous, but if it keeps me safe, I'm fine with it. Unless someone else tipped the police off and truly wanted to stay anonymous.

"Wow," Sami whispers. "Did you know about this?"

I look up from my phone. "I knew there were questions surrounding their possible involvement," I tell her. "Have you seen Max today?"

Sami looks up from reading the latest Twitter gossip. "Not yet."

I'm dying to know what's going on. Maybe I should call the detective? It's totally possible that Max could still be with him.

I excuse myself and go to my office to call him. He doesn't answer so I leave a message. I can only imagine how busy he is right now. I take a few deep breaths. The good news is this gives me hope that there is a light at the end of this tunnel. I just hope there's enough evidence to prove who really did this.

The next few hours are busy. I spend most of my time in the lobby assisting Sami with questions and concerns from guests. The on-site officers do a great job of keeping the press out of the lobby, and it's such a relief to have them here.

Max finally shows up after I return to my office. Without thinking, I jump up from my desk and run toward him. I throw my arms around him and feel his arms tighten around me.

"I wasn't expecting that kind of a greeting," he says into my hair.

I quickly pull away, but thankfully he doesn't completely let go of me.

"I'm sorry. When I didn't hear from you, I started to freak out. I'm so afraid that something is going to happen to someone else I care about."

The corner of his mouth curls up. At this point, I'm beyond worrying about everything I say and do.

"I was in such a rush this morning that I left my phone at home. I'm sorry I worried you."

I feel my cheeks get hot. So much for playing things cool. "What's happening?" I ask, hoping to change the subject. "What did the detective say?"

Max sits down in the chair, and I sit down right next to him. He tells me that Alfie admitted to trying to cover up Peyton's death, but is still insisting it was an accident. He claims they were talking at the top of the stairs, and she lost her balance when she tried to walk away. He's standing by his story that he panicked, and that's the reason he tampered with the video footage of her fall.

"Did he say anything about Phoebe?"

He shakes his head. "No. But they are laying it on pretty hard. Detective Cain still thinks the two deaths are linked somehow."

I sigh. "It's all over Twitter that James and Raven are now officially suspects in Phoebe's death."

He nods. "They are, thanks to you, but like Alfie, they're also claiming their innocence. And now that there's a question about James' alibi, the police haven't been able to get in touch with the family member they spoke to, and the number has been disconnected."

I sigh loudly.

He reaches over and puts his hand on my arm. A jolt shoots through my body. "They're getting a little bit closer to the truth every day."

He doesn't move his hand, and I don't move my arm. Neither of says anything for a few seconds.

"It feels good to have someone worry about me though," he says finally.

I smile. "I really was."

"I'm sorry I had to cancel on you this morning. I didn't want to."

I shrug. "It's okay, as long as you make it up to me."

He raises his eyebrows. "I think I can do that. How about a coffee rain check?"

All of a sudden Joelle's words flash through my mind. It doesn't matter though. It's too late, I'd already started falling for Max before I talked to her, and I don't think I'll be able to stop it.

"I probably have a million emails to get through," he adds, still not moving from his chair.

"I'm sure you do. It's been a busy morning around here, but Sami has things under control at the desk. I've been helping everywhere I'm needed."

He flashes me another brilliant smile. "I'm sure you're doing an outstanding job."

Ahhh ... our chemistry is officially off the charts. Before I can get a grip on what's happening, Max leans in toward me. Our lips are now inches apart, and so begins the internal battle within my soul.

Every cell in my body is screaming at me. I want Max to kiss me more than anything. At the same time, I've witnessed what can happen when two people in our work positions get involved.

My nostrils fill with the scent of Max's cologne, and before I can recall my last thoughts, or where I am, or what year it is ... his lips are on mine. Our kiss starts off slow and cautious but quickly becomes more urgent. All worries, concerns, and fears disappear as I savor every moment of being close to this gorgeous man.

His hands gently cup my face, and I wrap my arms around his neck. It's very obvious that we've both been craving this kind of intimacy.

After what feels like several minutes, our lips part and our foreheads touch. We're both breathless, and I close my eyes and try to gather my thoughts.

Unfortunately, Max gathers his before I'm able to do so. "I'm sorry. I shouldn't have done that," he exclaims.

That's definitely not the response I was hoping for and quite the opposite of how I was feeling. I feel my face fall, and Max must notice.

"Casey … I didn't mean to say it like that."

I fold my arms defensively. "Really? How did you mean to say it?"

He runs his fingers nervously through his hair. "I wanted to kiss you more than anything, believe me. I've wanted to do that since the first day I met you …"

I sense a "but" coming. "But?"

"At first, I was confident I could keep things professional between us, but the more I spend time with you, the more I want to be with you."

I'm so confused. "What are you trying to say?" I ask, not making any effort to hide my frustration.

He sighs. "And as much as I want to be with you right now and see where this goes, I don't want all the other distractions. I want to be all in with you, and I believe that together we can help make The Fountain Rose everything it can be."

I look down at the floor. As much as I don't like it, he's one hundred percent right.

"I don't want to slow things down. Trust me," he insists.

I really want to believe him. At the same time, that stupid Joelle and her words are creeping back into my mind. Which reminds me that I don't know much about Max or his past other than he's managed many hotels. That being said, there's a high probability that I'm not the first co-worker he's been attracted to, and I need to remind myself that getting attached to him could very well blow up in my face. I just hope he's not preying on my vulnerability. Maybe this is what he does—he swoops in, saving hotels and the lonely women in them.

He's about to say something else when his cell phone rings.

"You better get that."

He looks longingly at me. "This is Max. Yes, give me a few minutes."

I'm pretty sure our conversation is finished, so I stand up and walk around the desk toward my chair.

He ends the call and looks at me. "Can we talk later? I feel terrible leaving things like this."

I shrug my shoulders and try to act unfazed. "You shouldn't because you're absolutely right. We need to take a few steps back until we get this place up and running again."

He gives me a nod and stands up.

I pretend to be enthralled by my computer screen.

"Casey, there's one more thing."

"Yes?" I reply nonchalantly.

"As soon as this is all over, I hope to pick up where we left off earlier."

And with that, he's gone. I let out a low growl and bang my head against the back of my chair.

I think about the information Max just told me. So, Alfie claims he was talking to Peyton at the top of the stairs, and she fell? I wonder if they were talking about Phoebe. I still think he's leaving something out. And I still believe that she found something out either about him being in a relationship with Phoebe or about her death.

It's time for this case to be solved. Not only for justice but for my own sanity.

Chapter Twenty-Six

*W*hen I arrive in the lobby the next day, Max is talking to Belinda at the front desk. She looks exhausted, which isn't surprising, considering she's been working a lot of extra shifts.

"Good morning."

"Good morning, Casey," Max says.

Belinda barely acknowledges me. "My shift is officially over," she says with a yawn. "Unless you need me to do anything else?"

Clearly, she's speaking to Max, not me. She would never give me the satisfaction of her asking me if I need anything.

"I think we've got it under control. You go home and get some rest. Thank you again for everything. You're a star."

Belinda nods and then gives me a smug look before leaving me and Max alone for the first time since our conversation yesterday.

"How are you doing this morning?" he asks.

"I'm tired but somewhat relieved that the walls are finally closing in on Alfie, James, and Raven."

He gives me a wistful look. "Yes. But we shouldn't let our guards down yet, not until this is all over."

I agree. I can tell he feels uneasy. This is definitely taking a toll on all of us here at the hotel.

We both stand in silence, stealing glances at each other. One thing is for sure, the attraction is still going strong between us.

"Well, have a good morning. I'll check in later." He turns and walks away without a second look. Hmmm … he definitely meant what he said about taking things slowly.

It's been a quiet, uneventful morning at the hotel, and it feels glorious. I make myself busy with organizing my office and getting rid of the remainder of Joelle's things. I almost vomit when I find a bag of unmentionables in the back of a bottom drawer. It dawns on me that I don't know what transpired in this office during her tenure as the director of customer relations.

I'm searching online for new desks when my phone rings.

"Casey Cooper."

"Casey, it's Mikenzie," she whispers. "I have to talk to you."

"Mikenzie, why are you whispering?"

"It's very important. I found out some information about Phoebe, and you need to hurry."

A chill runs through my body. On any other day, I would think that she was being her usual dramatic self, but today, it doesn't feel that way.

"What's wrong? Tell me where you are."

"Can you meet me at the Ambassador Suite? We have to talk in private."

My heart begins to race. "What? Why there?"

"Trust me. I'll explain when we meet. Hurry." She hangs up before I have the chance to reply.

I hold the phone tightly in my hand.

What information could she possibly have about Phoebe? My mind quickly runs through different scenarios. Maybe this has to do with Alfie's older girlfriend? Or what if she has information on Raven's claims that she was Phoebe's sister?

My stomach twists into knots. Maybe she took the package after all?

I'm about to leave my office when my phone rings again. This time it's Kendall.

"Hey, can I call you back in a few?" I ask urgently.

"Sure. I just wanted to check in on you. Is everything okay?"

I tell her about Mikenzie's phone call.

"Casey, you need to be careful," she warns.

216 • MELISSA BALDWIN

"I am being careful. This place is crawling with security right now. It's probably safer than it's ever been."

"Okay." She doesn't sound convinced.

"Mikenzie says she has information about Phoebe, and I need to find out what it is."

"Fine. Just call me back. If I don't answer, just shoot me a text. My break is almost over."

"Deal." I quickly hang up and slide my phone into my pocket. I make my way to the place where Phoebe took her last breath. Hopefully, I will finally get the answers I've been looking for.

When I arrive on the twenty-seventh floor, a familiar feeling of sadness comes over me. It's eerily quiet, and I hesitate when I get off the elevator. We made the decision to not use the floor again until the investigation was closed, just in case the police needed access to it.

I stop in the doorway and look down the hall for Mikenzie. Typical. She tells me to hurry, but she's still not here. I wait on her for a few minutes before deciding to enter the suite.

I walk inside and then jump about ten feet in the air when I see Belinda sitting on the couch.

I stop. "Belinda? What are you doing here? I thought you already left after your shift."

She shakes her head, ignoring my question. "Casey, you really should fix your scarf. How many times have I told you that you need to make a good impression on our guests?"

Really? She's still reprimanding me about this damn scarf?

"What are *you* doing here?" she asks.

Me?

"I got an urgent call from Mikenzie to meet her here."

She rolls her eyes. "I got the same call from her. That girl is so dramatic. Ruby Carson—it's so ridiculous that she uses an alias because no one gives a damn about that girl. Those actresses are all the same," she says, sitting up straight and crossing her ankles. "Don't you agree, Casey? They're all spoiled, entitled, and think they're better than the rest of us. I would've never acted like that." She pauses. "And despite what you think, Phoebe Phord was the worst. Oh, the stories I could tell you."

Phoebe?

I suddenly feel a sense of urgency to get out of this room as quick as I can.

"Belinda, you're not making any sense," I say, as I head back toward the door.

"I wasn't finished talking!" Belinda yells. "Don't you want to wait for Mikenzie? I mean, it *is* your job to look after our guests. Especially when they're having an issue."

What is she rambling on about? I stop in my tracks, and when I flip around, she's holding a gun, and it's pointed directly at me.

Chapter Twenty-Seven

"Belinda, what are you doing?" I ask, my voice trembling. Suddenly it all becomes clear. Belinda was involved in Phoebe's death all along—she's the missing piece of the puzzle.

"I was trying to tell you a story, and once again you think you're too good to listen to me. It's really very rude of you to just leave one of your co-employees in the middle of a conversation. I often question your leadership skills."

My hands start to shake as I hold them up. "I've never thought I was too good to listen to you."

She stands up and begins to walk toward me. "Oh, right. That's why you roll your eyes every time I give you advice. You've never taken me seriously—but maybe you will now."

"Belinda, let's—"

"Get in there!" she shouts, pointing to the bedroom with the gun.

Without a word, I do as I'm told. When I walk into the bedroom, I find Mikenzie gagged and tied up on the floor. She's crying and lets out a muffled scream. Belinda obviously used Mikenzie to lure me here.

"Ruby, I told you to stop your whining," Belinda says in a theatrical voice.

She pushes me to the ground next to Mikenzie. I move as close to the wall as I can possibly get as I watch her pull over a chair and sit in front of me.

"Casey, why are you always in my way?" she asks calmly. *Too* calm. "First, you become best friends with Phoebe Phord, who happens to be one of the most heinous people I've ever met. Or I should say *was* one of the most heinous people I've ever met."

Seriously? This woman has a gun pointed at me, and now she's talking about heinous people?

"Then you take the job that I should have gotten. I reported Joelle and Colton the second I had the concrete proof that they were sleeping together all over this place. I was finally going to be noticed and get the job I worked so hard for, but no, you had to swoop in and take it out from under me."

She lets out a slow and controlled breath before she continues.

"But then you go and start tipping off the police and snooping in the security offices for answers about your precious Phoebe. You just couldn't leave well enough alone."

"I knew Phoebe didn't kill herself," I say calmly. "I was—"

She waves the gun around carelessly, causing my heart to pound against my chest. "I believe I am still talking." She shakes her head in frustration. "As if all of that wasn't enough. Then you take what rightfully belongs to my son and his girlfriend. He deserved more than he got, especially after putting up with that evil woman for as long as he did."

Her son? James!

I feel my mouth drop open. This is why she kept details about her son's life a secret. He told Phoebe that his mother was a fan of Phoebe's and that she died. He used that lie to get close to her. That explains why it seemed strange that Belinda's son never came to see her—he was here all the time. Wow. I remember when he came to talk to me the day after Phoebe died. Belinda made a comment about the reporters harassing him. This is crazy.

"James is your son. The son you always talk about. And Raven is his girlfriend?"

She smiles proudly. "He's gorgeous, isn't he? Takes after his father. The man was an ass, but we made a beautiful child."

This woman has gone mad.

Phoebe's assistant is Belinda's precious one-and-only child. I can't even count how many times Belinda told me about his very important job and what a dedicated and loyal son he was. I guess I was wrong about him blowing her off. She wasn't lying when she said he promised to take care of her. Did he think he was going to inherit Phoebe's fortune and set his mother up for life?

"So, your son was working for Phoebe to get access to her money? And you, his mother, confirmed his alibi?"

She gets a familiar gleam in her eye that I've seen in the past. "He was taking care of family business that day."

My mind is spinning as I try to make sense of what I'm hearing. James was working for Phoebe, and obviously Raven and him are together. Could it be true that they were trying to exploit her since day one? With James being so close to Phoebe, Raven had another way to worm into Phoebe's life, especially since Phoebe wanted nothing to do with her.

"Did Raven orchestrate this whole plan so she could get her hands on Phoebe's money? Or did you and James seek her out? That's it, isn't it? One way or another, you were all going to get her fortune. Either through her cousin, or you thought she was actually going to leave it to James, so you murdered her."

Belinda shakes her head. "My son and Raven met by chance before he started working for her. We realized who she was when she told us her tragic story about her family shunning the poor girl her whole life. They were terrible to her. Phoebe and Raven may not have been sisters, but she was family, and you don't treat family that way."

I shake my head in disbelief. "You took the package too. It contained the proof that they weren't sisters, and you took it so no one would find out the truth, and so you would have a backup plan just in case Phoebe didn't leave James her money."

This is awful. Phoebe really cared about James. She let him in, and the whole time, he was plotting to take everything from her, including her life.

"Everyone put Phoebe Phord up on a pedestal. She wasn't the angel you think she was. She would do whatever it took to get what she wanted."

"I never thought she was—"

"Oh, sure you did," she interrupts. "'She was the sister I never had,' blah, blah … 'We bonded over no family,' blah, blah …"

I look over at Mikenzie who has tears streaming down her face and is now shaking uncontrollably.

"Did Phoebe tell you that I was supposed to have that leading role on *Love and Eternity?*" Belinda asks.

Wait. Suddenly I remember the article I found in Alfie's office. He must've gotten it from her.

"You're the actress Phoebe beat out for that role," I say.

She glares at me. "She pretended she didn't know who I was, but I know she remembered me. She avoided me every chance she got because she stole that role from me, and she knew it."

I take a deep breath. "First you tell me that James is your son, and now you're saying that you were up for the same role on that show as Phoebe?"

She lets out an unpleasant laugh. "Now do you see what I mean? I've been trying to tell you this story, but you didn't want to listen. You never stop talking, Casey. That's why you're here, because you never shut up."

She stretches her arms out in front of her, which brings the gun even closer to me. I lean up against the wall again, as far away as I can get.

"My sweet boy and Raven's meeting happened by chance. But I now know it was meant to be. Phoebe was finally going to get what she deserved. She had hurt both of us immensely, and James hated that. He's so loyal, truly a gentleman, so he stepped in to make things right."

I glance around the room and realize I'm right near the very spot I found Phoebe that day. Tears well up in my eyes, but I push them back. "How did you do it? Did she let you into her room? How did you force her to take those pills?"

She gives me a wicked smile. "Oh, that was easy. I told her I had her delivery, and she opened the door for me. When she saw the gun, she tried to run in here but tripped and dropped her bag. She was already all dressed up, so that was convenient. And then I told her that if she didn't take the pills, I would kill you. That should make you feel good, Casey. Maybe she really did care about you."

No!

The tears I was trying to fight make their way out of my eyes. I know now more than ever that she meant to leave the bracelet for me. She died because she thought it would save me. My hand is shaking as I put it to my mouth. I feel like I'm going to throw up.

"And what about Peyton?" I say through my tears.

Belinda teases her blonde hair with her free hand. "Peyton was an unforeseen complication. I told Alfred to stop messing with that little tramp. She was taking his attention away from me, and I needed him. I should have known he would screw everything up."

So, Belinda is the woman that Joelle was talking about, which means Alfie and her have been together all this time. No wonder Belinda had so much disdain for Peyton.

"Did you push her?"

She looks taken back. "No, I didn't push her. Stupid girl. She saw Alfred and me together, completely flipped out, and left. But, like you, she loves to hear herself talk. She just *had* to have the last word, so she came back. When Alfred tried to calm her down, she lost her balance. And then *bam!* She hit that floor hard, and it wasn't a pretty sight."

Wow. This woman is rotten to the core.

She lets out a frustrated sigh. "And then he totally caved and admitted he tried to cover up her fall. Can you believe how stupid he is?" She shrugs. "Oh well, I got what I needed from him. I was able to remove all traces of evidence from Phoebe's death by erasing all footage from that day, and just in case there were any further complications, I left that magazine article in his office."

She smiles proudly. "Our relationship served me well, being that I could have access to the office anytime I wanted to, and I convinced him I was fascinated with how the hotel's security system worked."

Belinda was using Alfie too. Maybe he hadn't meant to hurt Peyton after all. That must have been what Peyton wanted to talk to me about. She saw Alfie and Belinda together.

"Was it you who was following me in the parking lot too?"

This thought sends a shiver down my spine. I have no doubt she would have killed me if given the chance. She has a gun inches from my face right now. I need to keep her talking. It may be my only hope of survival.

She rolls her eyes. "You complicate things too much, Casey. You should've just done your job and stayed out of it." She grimaces. "You know, this is all your fault. If it weren't for you, nobody would've suspected that the fabulous Phoebe Phord didn't give in to all her demons. It was all so perfectly staged, exactly the way she would have wanted it. She was wearing stunning couture, and she even had the Emmys with her, the Emmys that should have been *mine*."

I guess James told the truth about one thing, he brought the Emmys to the hotel. I look into her eyes, and I finally see the years of rage and frustration that must have been building over time to bring her to this very moment.

"You had to be so insistent that Phoebe would never kill herself. Now the police have arrested everyone I love, and it's all because of you. I've lost everything I've ever cared about."

I look at Mikenzie, whose eyes are now closed.

"Belinda, you're not going to get away with this. They will catch up to you."

She laughs again. "Maybe I won't get away with it, and that's fine, as long as you get what you deserve. I don't have anything left. But you—" She begins to casually wave the gun around again. "You, Casey Cooper, have Phoebe's fortune."

I frown. "I never wanted Phoebe's money."

She sneers at me. "Sure you did. That's why you became best

friends with her. You manipulated your way into her life, and by doing that, you screwed my son."

Mikenzie starts thrashing around and kicking. Her mascara is now streaming down her face. She looks like she's in a scene from a horror movie.

"Oh, stop being so dramatic!" Belinda yells at her. "You're just another spoiled actress. Another person who put Phoebe Phord on a pedestal. Honestly, the way you acted like you were so close with Phoebe after she died. It was so pathetic. She didn't care about you either, and you practically got on the ground and kissed her feet." She lets out a wicked laugh. "Did you actually think being friends with Phoebe Phord was going to resuscitate your career? Keep dreaming, little girl, no one knows who you are anymore."

Belinda looks like she's becoming more deranged by the second. I have to do something before she kills Mikenzie and me both. Suddenly, I have an idea. I don't know if it will work, but I have to try.

Chapter Twenty-Eight

"*B*elinda, I think I know a way we can help each other. Just hear me out."

She narrows her eyes. "You want to help me? I'm supposed to believe you? Why?"

My heart races as she repositions the gun. I shrug my shoulders and wipe my tears. "Because I want justice for Phoebe, and because no matter what you've done, I know how much you love your son. I mean, come on, how many conversations have we had about him?"

She eyes me curiously. "He really is a good boy. Look at the lengths he's gone to help me," she continues. "He knows how difficult my life has been, and he's willing to do anything to help me, even become a slave to that horrible woman. He's a very loyal son."

Belinda's expression completely changes when she talks about James, and I can see she loves him, in her own twisted kind of way. Whatever. I need to use this to my advantage. She may see right through me, but I have to try.

"I can see that." I pause as I collect my thoughts. "Belinda, it was never my intention to cause you all this pain. I had no idea I would get Joelle's position, and although it may have seemed like I didn't listen to your suggestions, I really did. I did value your advice and experience. Honestly, there have been many times I've thought that you should have gotten the job."

Her face continues to soften, but she hasn't moved the gun, so until that thing is out of my face, I have to keep talking. "And you can ask Phoebe's attorney. I told him I wasn't sure I was taking all that money. I was as shocked as anyone by Phoebe's will."

She gives me a doubtful look. "But you haven't given it up yet."

I shake my head. "No … not yet. The truth is … I've been torn —all of Phoebe's fortune didn't bring her peace or happiness. I'm not sure I want that burden, and to be honest, I'm learning we weren't as close as I thought we were. I confided in her about the most personal aspects of my life. I thought we had bonded over lack of family, but she never even told me about Raven."

"Phoebe Phord only cared about herself," she says firmly.

"I'm starting to see that now. Maybe you're right about her."

I glance at Mikenzie, who's watching me carefully. Either she knows what I'm doing, or she thinks I'm the most horrible person on the planet. I'm just trying to get us out of this mess. And here goes nothing …

"And you ..." I raise my voice and point at Mikenzie. "You came to me, and we talked about Phoebe's tragic death, and you acted like you were devastated when all along, you were hoping to use her death and your pretend friendship to get your career back on track. You never cared about what happened to her, did you?"

Mikenzie continues to thrash around like a maniac.

I focus my attention back on Belinda, who's watching me intently.

"What if we make her confess to Phoebe's murder?" I ask, pointing at Mikenzie. "Think about it—Mikenzie Bronsyn, just another washed-up actress who was looking to profit off of Phoebe Phord. This could have been her brilliant idea from the start."

Belinda gives me a skeptical look.

"I want to make things right with you," I continue. "I'll give up Phoebe's money if that's what it takes."

Belinda's usual immaculate appearance is nowhere to be found. She now looks tired and completely disheveled. Clearly, she's had some sort of a break. "I don't know," she says, standing up. "I have to figure out my next move."

I can feel my body relax now that the gun is no longer in my face. This reprieve may only be temporary, but I'll take it.

"I'll give up my job. You can have it," I say.

She puts her hands to her head, bringing the gun next to her temple. "Stop talking, I need to think."

All of a sudden, my phone starts vibrating from my back

pocket. Thankfully, I turned off the ringer this morning. I try to figure out a way to answer it without Belinda noticing. Luckily, she's still pacing back and forth a few feet away from me. I'm still on the floor sitting against the wall, so I reach one hand behind me and start touching the screen.

"What are you doing?"

I pull my hand out from behind my back. "Nothing. I was just stretching," I say nervously.

She walks toward me and puts the gun back in my face. "Give it to me."

I reach into my pocket and grab my phone. Suddenly a huge burst of adrenaline takes over my body, and I throw the phone across the room. Belinda turns, and I jump up and tackle her.

The next few seconds are a blur, and then I hear the gunshot.

Chapter Twenty-Nine

I'm covering my head when I feel someone grab my arm. I let out an ear-piercing scream and pull away. Then I look up to see Max standing over me. I jump into his arms and begin to sob. As I begin to calm down and my blood pressure drops to a safe level, I look around the room. After I tackled Belinda, I heard the gun go off, but I don't see any blood.

"Did anyone get hurt when the gun went off?"

Max shakes his head. "Her finger must have been on the trigger because the bullet is lodged in the wall." He points to the wall above the bed. "She must have dropped the gun when she hit the ground. The police said she was reaching for it when they came in."

I gasp as I take in my surroundings. I see Belinda lying on the ground, her hands in handcuffs. Two police officers are standing over her. I see Detective Cain crouching down, talking to a completely shaken Mikenzie. Her hands are free, and she's talking a mile a minute, and then I see Ryan lingering by the door.

I must have had a moment of insanity when I thought it would be smart to tackle a deranged woman who was hell-bent on revenge. But my instinct took over, and I knew I had to do something if I was going to make it out alive. I begin to sob loudly again as I replay what just happened.

"It's okay. It's over," Max says as he runs his fingers through my hair.

"Belinda was behind the whole thing," I wail. "She hated Phoebe because she got the role on *Love and Eternity*. And James is her son."

I look at Belinda, who's still cuffed and now sitting up. She's completely still with an empty expression on her face. She looks eerily catatonic. I feel a wave of sadness come over me. She took another life, all because of jealousy and greed.

Max gently rubs my back.

My hands shake as I push my hair away from my face. "How did you know where we were?"

"Your roommate called the hotel and told me about you meeting with Mikenzie. She said you were supposed to call her back, but you never did. What were you thinking coming here alone?"

I shrug my shoulders. "I wanted to talk to her about Phoebe. I had no idea Belinda made her do it to lure me here."

I knew James had to be involved from day one, and it was easy to figure out when Raven showed up at just the right time, but *Belinda?* I never suspected that she was James' mother.

I throw my head back. "James manipulated Phoebe to get close to her so he could get revenge for his mother and Raven. He wanted to have her fortune and to please his mother so badly that he was willing to kill for it."

One thing is for certain—I don't want any of that money. Like I told Belinda, it never brought Phoebe any happiness … if anything, it led to her demise.

"Hey, Casey," Ryan says, joining us. "I just talked to Kendall and told her you were all right."

"Did you tell her that she saved my life? She's my guardian angel."

He blushes. "She is pretty great."

He clears his throat then excuses himself to talk to another officer. I'm sure this isn't the exact moment he wants to be gushing about how much he adores his girlfriend.

"She was about to shoot me," I sob. "She had that gun pointed at my face the entire time. I managed to get her to relax by telling her I would help her frame Mikenzie."

Max gives me a faint smile. "That was smart."

I huff. "It was the only thing I could think of. I know how much Belinda loves her son so I used that, and her dedication to this hotel, to make her trust me."

Max pushes a strand of hair out of my face. "You're so brave."

My heart begins to race again, only this time, it's not because I'm fearing for my life.

"How are you holding up, Ms. Cooper?" Detective Cain asks.

I drag my gaze away from Max, whose eyes are still fixed on me as well. "I'm just grateful this is finally over."

"I know you've been through a lot, but I do need to take your statement."

Max clears his throat. "I'll let you do that while I check on things downstairs."

No. I don't want you to go.

He looks at me and reaches for my hand. "I'll be back soon."

"Okay," I say, my voice weak.

I look at Mikenzie, who still looks completely distraught.

"I'm sorry," I tell her. "It was the only thing I could think of to distract her."

She nods. "I know. I'm glad you did it, but for a second, I actually believed you were serious. That was such good acting."

Mikenzie tells us about Belinda calling her and luring her to the Ambassador Suite. After she got her there, Belinda forced Mikenzie to call me.

"Can you tell me about everything that happened after you arrived?" Detective Cain asks.

I launch into my statement as I relive every detail about what happened from the moment I answered Mikenzie's phone call.

"How can people be so horrible?" I ask after Mikenzie leaves to get checked out.

He frowns. "I ask myself that question every day. Thank you for all you did to help us. Ms. Phord was lucky to have a friend like you. Which reminds me, I have something for you." He stops and reaches into his pocket. He pulls out Phoebe's bracelet, still inside a plastic bag.

"I was able to get this released, and I thought you would want to have it."

Once again, tears fill my eyes as I take it out of his hand. This makes me think about what Phoebe did to protect me.

One of the other police officers summons him away, leaving me alone for the first time since my ordeal.

As overwhelmed as I am right now, I feel like for the first time in weeks, I can breathe. Both Phoebe and Peyton are finally getting the justice they deserve, and the truth can now be told.

"Hey."

I look up to see Max standing next to me. A feeling of peace comes over me like it always does when he's around. "Thanks for coming back."

He holds out his hand. "I told you I would."

I sigh. "I'm ready to go home, and I could really use a cup of tea."

"So, do you think you will finally take some time off?"

I shrug my shoulders. "Maybe for a day or two."

He raises his eyebrows.

"Or maybe a week."

"That sounds more like it," he says with a smile.

Chapter Thirty

"Seriously, you guys don't have to fuss over me anymore!" I exclaim.

It's been almost two days since everything went down at the hotel, and Kendall and Jenn have been babysitting me. It's getting to the point now where they are fighting over doing things for me, and it's making me crazy.

"Yes, we do," Kendall says. "Especially after what you've been through. You did the same for me, remember?"

I rub my temples as they continue to fluff my pillow and adjust my blanket.

Jenn leaves and returns a few seconds later with a cup of tea. "Do you want me to braid your hair?"

Braid my hair? *This isn't a slumber party.*

"I'm okay right now. I love you both for wanting to take care of me, but I promise I'm feeling better."

Thankfully, the doorbell rings to distract them from me. Jenn runs out to answer it.

"She won't leave," Kendall says under her breath.

I let out a giggle.

Jenn rushes into my room with a huge smile on her face. "Casey, there's a gorgeous man here to see you."

Max is here?

Kendall raises her eyebrows and gives me a sly look. "Do you want us to leave? I could run to the studio."

Jenn nods her head and gives Kendall a wicked smile. "And I could run a few errands."

At least they are finally agreeing on something, and they're going to leave.

I hop out of bed and run my fingers through my hair. Thankfully, I just took a shower this morning. I make my way to the living room where Max is now sitting on the couch. There is a beautiful bouquet of wild flowers resting on the coffee table.

"Hey."

He rises to his feet as soon as he sees me. "Hi. I'm sorry I didn't call first."

"Max, can you stay with her for a few minutes?" Jenn asks. "I have a few errands to run."

"I'm fine," I say at the same time Max says, "No problem."

A few seconds later, Kendall comes out of her room and announces that she has to go to the studio for a little while.

I roll my eyes. It's so obvious what they're doing. Within a few minutes, they are both gone, and I let out a cheer. "Finally. Those two haven't left my side, and as much as I appreciate them for wanting to take care of me, I need a break. So, thank you for coming over and for the beautiful flowers."

I sit down, and he follows my lead.

"I know I could have called, but … well, the truth is, I wanted to see you."

Yes, yes, yes!

He nervously shifts around on the couch. "I know there's a lot going on right now, but I really wanted to tell you something. When I walked into that hotel room after hearing the gunshot and saw you on the ground … I don't know how to put into words how I felt in that moment." He gently pushes a strand of my hair behind my ear. "It really shook me that you could've been hurt."

"I was so glad you were there. You make me feel safe."

"Good." He sighs. "We have a lot to figure out, especially at the hotel. I'm in the process of hiring a new assistant manager. Jeremy has worked with me at a few properties, and he's great in a crisis. I should have brought him on sooner, but my ego got in the way. I wanted to be the one to step in and rescue The Fountain Rose, but I'm slowly learning that I can't do this on my own. And I need to have more in my life than my career."

"So do I," I say. "That's something I've learned from Phoebe's situation. Her whole life was her career, and look where that left her."

Max reaches over and takes my hand. "I meant what I said about us taking things slowly. But I want to see where this can go. And I know I insisted you take time off, but I hate it when you're not there."

I laugh. "Well, with the way things are going around here, I might be back at work tomorrow."

He moves his face closer to mine. "I'm okay with that."

Neither of us says another word, and I fall into his arms.

My heart is beating so fast as I sit in the chair across from Judd Dawson's desk. This moment has been a long time coming, but I'm finally ready to do it. As usual, his outfit doesn't disappoint. Today he's wearing a white suit with an emerald green T-shirt underneath it.

"I have to say I'm surprised by this, Ms. Cooper," he says. "Phoebe really wanted you to have her estate."

"I know she did, which is why I'm taking just enough to pay off my credit card. I want the remainder of her money to go to a good cause, to help children who don't have families of their own. I think Phoebe's legacy should help others, not just me."

He shakes his head. "Well, this is certainly a first in my career."

I shrug my shoulders. "As tempting as it is to keep it, I've seen the devastation that the desire for her fortune has caused.

Two beautiful people are dead, and three others are facing serious charges ranging from extortion to murder. I want to have a clean break and move on with my life. I think Phoebe would understand."

He sighs loudly. "Okay, I'll draw up the papers and have them ready for you to sign in a few days."

I hold out my hand and shake his. "Thank you, Judd. It's been a pleasure."

I'm about to walk out of his office when he stops me. "Phoebe really did consider you her family."

I nod. "And I felt the same way."

As I make my way to the hotel, I think about Phoebe and everything I've learned since her death. I know she wasn't perfect, and she had struggles just like the rest of us, but she was there when I needed a friend, and I will always appreciate her for that.

As soon as I enter the lobby, I feel a sense of peace. I immediately notice that the police officers are gone, and I recognize the excitement that I haven't felt here in a long time.

Max scheduled a big meeting for this afternoon to talk about our upcoming changes and to introduce our new assistant manager and the new security team.

Sami is talking to a muscular bald guy I assume is Jeremy. She looks up and waves at me. "Welcome back, Casey," she says warmly. "Have you met our new assistant manager yet?

"Thank you. It's nice to meet you. Welcome to The Fountain Rose." I wave my hand around like I'm on a talk show.

He gives me a big toothy grin. "It's good to be here. I told Maxwell he should've brought me on sooner. I can fight crime with the best of them."

We all laugh.

"He says you're cool in a crisis," I tell him. "We definitely could've used you around here."

"Next time."

I cringe at the thought. "Hopefully there isn't a next time for quite a while."

"I second that," a voice says from behind me.

I turn around to see Max, in all his superhero glory, standing behind me. My stomach does a flip, but I manage to keep my excitement to myself.

"Welcome back, Casey."

I beam. "It feels good to be back."

"Okay, enough standing around," he says with a smile. "It's time to bring this hotel back to life."

We all snap to attention and disperse. I head to my office to type up my report for our meeting. A few minutes later, Max appears in my doorway.

"I just wanted to give you a proper welcome back," he teases, putting his hands in his pockets.

I shake my head. "Remember, Mr. Sheridan, we're taking

things slow. Our first priority is the guests of The Fountain Rose Resort." I touch Phoebe's bracelet, which now has a permanent place on my wrist, and I'm reminded how much her friendship meant to me.

"You're absolutely right," he says.

"Yes," I say with a smile. "Because our guests mean the world to us."

Epilogue

I take a look around at the lobby, which is buzzing with photographers and guests. I smile to myself. This time, we *want* the cameras flashing.

It's been five months since my harrowing ordeal with Belinda, and things are finally looking up. We went through a rough patch after everything went down, and I admit, I was worried that the end of our hotel was near. We continued to lose business even after the murders of Phoebe and Peyton were solved.

I truly thought all was lost until Kendall came home one night from the studio talking about needing a location for her movie's wrap party.

I got on the phone with Max immediately, and tonight is the night. I've never attended a wrap party, and it's everything I imagined it would be. Good food, celebrities, flashing cameras, and even a red carpet.

The Fountain Rose Resort is back in the limelight, and it's slowly becoming the desired hotel destination it once was.

In other news, the life story of Phoebe Phord is finally becoming a movie, and guess who's producing it—Kendall's film company, Blossom Studios. Phoebe's name has been all over the media after her fortune was donated to foster homes and adoption agencies around the country. I know without a doubt that I made the right decision when it came to that money.

Speaking of family, I've been in touch with both my parents and in the process of making plans to see them. It's time for me to move on from the pain of the past, and reconnecting with family is part of that.

In true Max fashion, he stepped in and helped to bring The Fountain Rose back to life. And since he arrived, he's also brought me back to life. We're continuing to take our relationship slowly as we both try to balance our career and personal lives.

I look around the lobby where I see Kendall, Ryan, Jenn, and Max talking to reporters and drinking champagne. The Fountain Rose Resort isn't just a place of work to me.

This is my home.

These people are my family, and they mean the world to me.

The End

Poison in Paradise: a tropical romantic
mystery

Buy now or read for free with your Kindle Unlimited
Membership!

Life on the open seas is everything Lexi Walker ever wanted!
Her position as the part-time lifeguard and part-time Port
Adventures coordinator for Epic Cruise Line has her
traveling around the world and living her dream. And she has
high hopes that her latest trip to the tropical Bahamas will be
nothing short of magical.

Hopes that are dashed all too quickly.

What starts as a chance connection with a friend from her
past, who is sailing on Epic to celebrate her recent marriage,
turns into a deadly tragedy when Lexi finds the groom dead
in a resort's hot tub! Was it an accident? Or something more
sinister? Suddenly Lexi finds herself thrust into a potential
murder investigation where everyone is hiding something

and no one seems innocent. Between trying to help the widow in desperate need of support, sifting through the victim's friends and family who are anything but grieving, and trying to prove to her boss, the way-too-tempting Jack Carson, that she's an asset and not a liability to Epic Cruise Line, Lexi has her hands full.

"Melissa Baldwin's highly imaginative story is one filled with fun, excitement and romance."

—Readers Favorite Book Reviews

Dear Reader

I hope you enjoyed *Room Service and Murder*. Please take a few minutes to leave a review on Amazon, and don't forget to check out *Movie Scripts and Madness*, the first book in the Madness and Murder Mysteries series.

Love my books? Join my reader group on Facebook!

Visit my website for updates, and stay tuned for my next book coming soon.

AuthorMelissaBaldwin.com

Acknowledgments

To my wonderful editor Wendi Baker, thank you for all your time, encouragement, and patience. I owe this book to you!

To Sue Traynor, you've done it again. Another brilliant cover.

To Karan Eleni, thank you for always being there to lend a hand. You always have the answers I need.

To Paula Bothwell, thank you for your willingness to read my books and for your support.

To my husband and my daughter. Thank you for encouraging me not to give up. I love you.

About the Author

Melissa Baldwin is an avid runner, planner obsessed, and has always had a love for writing. She is a wife, mother, and journal keeper who took her creativity to the next level by fulfilling her dream with her debut novel, *An Event to Remember ... or Forget*. Melissa writes about charming, ambitious, and real women. She is a best-selling author of sixteen Romantic Comedy and Cozy Mystery novels and novellas.

When she isn't deep in the writing zone, this multi-tasking master organizer is busy spending time with her family, chauffeuring her daughter, traveling, running, indulging in fitness, and taking a Disney Cruise every now and then.

Connect with Melissa at
authormelissabaldwin.com

Made in the USA
Columbia, SC
02 February 2021

32210197R00143